CLAUDIA AND THE GREAT SEARCH

I began looking at the picture of Janine and me again. I looked at them carefully. We don't look a bit alike now, but maybe we'd looked alike when we were little, when our parents dressed us in matching clothes and gave us the same haircuts.

Nope. We barely looked related . . .

A funny feeling crept into my stomach. I replaced the photo albums on the shelves . . .

All of a sudden it dawned on me. I knew. I just *knew*. I was *adopted*.

Why are Claudia and Janine *so* different? And where are all Claudia's baby pictures? Claudia is determined to find out the truth. Is she who thinks she is, or is she . . . adopted!

Also in the Babysitters Club series:

Look out for:

Babysitters' Specials:

Look out for:

CLAUDIA AND THE GREAT SEARCH

Ann M. Martin

Hippo Books
Scholastic Children's Books
London

Scholastic Children's Books,
Scholastic Publications Ltd,
7-9 Pratt Street, London NW1 0AE, UK

Scholastic Inc.,
730 Broadway, New York, NY 10003, USA

Scholastic Canada Ltd,
123 Newkirk Road, Richmond Hill,
Ontario, Canada L4C 3G5

Ashton Scholastic Pty Ltd,
P O Box 579, Gosford, New South Wales,
Australia

Ashton Scholastic Ltd,
Private Bag 1, Penrose, Auckland,
New Zealand

First published in the US by Scholastic Inc., 1990
First published in the UK by Scholastic Publications Ltd, 1992

Text copyright © Ann M. Martin, 1990
THE BABYSITTERS CLUB is a registered trademark of Scholastic Inc.

ISBN 0 590 55131 0

Typeset in Plantin by Contour Typesetters, Southall, London
Printed by Cox & Wyman Ltd, Reading, Berks.

10 9 8 7 6 5 4 3 2

This book is for Jane,
who is my sister
(I think)

1st CHAPTER

Click, click, click.

I watched the second hand on the clock in the front of my classroom work its way slowly around and around the dial. When the room was silent, as it was then, every time the hand on the clock jumped forward one second, it made a clicking sound.

It was a faithful old clock. You could depend on it. Every afternoon it clicked its way from 1:10 to 1:51, and when that second hand clicked over to the twelve at precisely 1:51, the bell rang—and I was released from the horrors of the science lesson.

I absolutely can't stand science, especially biology, which was what we were studying. I couldn't keep track of all those terms—cell and nucleus, species and phylum and genus, RNA and DNA and who knows what else. You know what's really stupid? The word *species*. If you have two different kinds of

1

animal or something, then you have two species. But if you have only one kind, then you still have a *species*. Why not a specie? Or a specy? You don't have two cats and one cats.

Oh, well.

Click, click, click.

We were supposed to be reading the instructions for an experiment we were going to perform in the lesson that day. Now there's another stupid thing. Year after year, the same teacher makes his pupils perform the same experiments. Well, if the experiments have been done so many times before, how can they still be experiments? The teacher *knows* what's going to happen. I thought experimenting meant trying *new* things to see what would happen. We weren't experimenting at all. We were play-acting.

But none of this really mattered. I, Claudia Kishi, was just biding my time. I wasn't going to have to perform the experiment that day. I was simply waiting for the clock to click to 1:20. Then I was going to ... *leave early*! I couldn't wait.

Well, I couldn't wait to leave the lesson. I *could* wait for what I had to do after I'd left. What did I have to do? I had to go to an awards ceremony at which my older sister, Janine the Genius, was going to be given some big honour. As if she isn't always being awarded for something. Every time I

2

turn round she's getting another certificate or prize, or she's got all A grades again.

My sister and I really are different. It's hard to believe we're related. I never get awards or win prizes. Okay, I've received a few awards, but they were for my art. I'm proud of the awards, and my parents are, too, I think, but Janine really *stands out* when it comes to schoolwork. Maybe I should tell you a little bit about my family so you can understand things better.

To begin with, there are four people in my family—Mum, Dad, Janine, and me. Janine is sixteen and a junior at Stoneybrook High School, otherwise known as SHS. (We live in Stoneybrook, Connecticut.) I am thirteen and in the eighth grade at Stoneybrook Middle School, or SMS. There used to be a fifth person in our family—my grandmother Mimi. Mimi and I were very close. I could tell her anything. She always listened to me, and she didn't care that I'm not such a brilliant pupil. She really liked my art, too. But now Mimi's gone. She died a little while ago. I miss her a lot.

Our family is Japanese-American. Janine and I were born here in Stoneybrook, though. We've never even been to Japan. My dad is a partner in an investment firm in Stamford, which is a city nearby. My mum is the head librarian at our local public library. I'm stupid and Janine is a genuis. Oh, okay. I know that isn't true. I mean,

3

about my being stupid. According to my teachers I'm very bright. I just don't apply myself. I have a little trouble concentrating, and frankly, school doesn't interest me. But art does. I love everything about art. And I'm good at it. I can sculpt, paint, sketch, make collages and jewellery, you name it. I'm not bragging. This is just the way things are.

Then there's Janine. She doesn't care about anything *except* school. She especially likes computers and science. She's a true and honest genius. She has a genius IQ— over 150. She's so clever that even though she's only at high school, she goes to some classes at the community college. She's been doing that for two years now.

Janine and I are as different as night and day.

But back to the science lesson.

Click, click, click. Just when everyone had finished reading the instructions for the "experiment", the second hand on the clock struck 1:20.

I jumped up.

"I have to go now," I reminded my teacher.

"Okay. See you tomorrow, Claudia," he replied. (It was only Monday, the beginning of a new week of amoebas and paramecia and other biological things.)

I gathered up my things, dashed out of

4

the classroom and to my locker, where I put away my science text book, took out two other books, and grabbed my jacket. Then I raced to the front of SMS.

My father was waiting for me.

"Hi," I said, as I climbed into his car.

"Hi, darling," he replied.

Dad drove through Stoneybrook to the high school. We were going to meet my mother there. I couldn't believe that both of my parents had left their jobs for this awards ceremony. (Well, Mum was going back to hers afterwards, since it's so close by, but Dad wasn't. Stamford is too far away.)

When we reached the high school, Dad parked our car and we walked to the main entrance of the building. There we found Mum, Peaches, and Russ waiting for us. Peaches and Russ are my aunt and uncle. (Peaches is Mum's sister.) I love them. They are totally cool and funny. Real characters. Russ is American. I mean, he's not Japanese. And he's the one who came up with the name Peaches. Mimi gave Mum and Peaches Japanese names, but Russ started calling my aunt Peaches, and it sort of stuck. Now everybody calls her Peaches. And everybody just calls Russ, Russ. Not even Russell, which is his full first name. Janine and I don't even call them Aunt Peaches and Uncle Russ. They're Peaches and Russ to the whole world. They don't have any children (I think maybe they *can't* have any), but I wish they did. They would be brilliant parents.

Mum and Dad and Peaches and Russ and I greeted each other with hugs and handshakes and hellos. Then we went inside the building, and a pupil directed us to the main hall. When we got there, Mum told a teacher that we'd come to see Janine Kishi receive her award.

"Oh, you're *Janine's* family," said the teacher in an awed way. "I'm *so* glad to meet you. *Please* follow me to the re*served* section of the main hall. You must be *aw*fully proud of Janine."

Gush, gush, gush.

Honestly, this teacher, whoever he was, was falling all over himself about Janine. Okay, so she'd won another award. Big deal.

But it *was* a big deal. I mean, the high school *made* it a big deal. The teacher led us to a section of seats at the front of the main hall which had been roped off with gold braid. Tasteful signs that read RESERVED hung from the braid. The teacher made a big show of unroping the third row for us, and my family and I filed in and sat down. We could see Janine and the other kids who'd be getting awards sitting in the first row.

"Congratulations," said the teacher as he left us.

"Thank you," replied Mum and Dad at the same time. They were beaming.

Soon the ceremony began. First the school band played. Then the Head Teacher said a few words, then the Student Council Chairman spoke, and finally the Deputy Head Teacher stepped onto the stage. She was going to present the awards.

I looked around the main hall. It was packed. All the kids at the school were there, as well as all the teachers, and several other families like mine. There weren't enough seats for everyone, so some of the kids were sitting on the windowsills, and the teachers were standing in the aisles. Even the balcony was filled. I looked round for any kids I knew—in particular, the older brothers of my friend Kristy—but I couldn't find them.

Anyway, Dad nudged me and said, "Pay attention, darling."

I faced forward and tried to concentrate.

The Deputy Head was handing out the awards. First she presented one for excellence in English, then one for excellence in maths, three for excellence in foreign languages, and one for outstanding leadership qualities.

Finally she said, "And now I am proud—no, I am *hon*oured—to present the final award. It's a very special award, and has been granted only once before. That was ten years ago, to a senior pupil. This time it will be presented to a *junior* pupil, as the most accomplished science pupil at the *community* *college*, where this pupil has been going to classes for two years, in addition to her classes here at the high school. Janine Kishi, please will you come forward and accept your award?"

My sister, looking nervous, stood up from her place in the first row and made her way to the stage. She didn't trip going up the steps or anything, and she accepted her plaque and a cheque for $250 very graciously. Before she left the stage she turned, smiled at Mum and Dad and Peaches and Russ and me, and then went back to her seat.

The ceremony was over.

But the nightmare had begun.

Can you believe it? All these people—kids, teachers, my family—ran up to Janine and started congratulating her. She was absolutely surrounded, all hemmed in, but she looked as if she were loving every minute of it.

Guess what? A photographer and a reporter from the *Stoneybrook News* were there. The photographer took some pictures of Janine holding up her plaque and the cheque. Then the reporter turned to my family and began asking us questions.

"Your sister is awfully clever," he said to me. (Duh.) "Are you a genius, too?"

Me? A genius? "Uh, well, I'm—"

Before I could tell him about my art, he turned to my mother and asked if she were proud of Janine.

Gosh, what probing questions.

While that was happening, Janine's bio-chemistry teacher at the high school was talking to Dad. Then she said to me, "You're Janine's sister?"

I nodded.

"Well, I'll certainly be looking forward to having you in my class one day—if you're anything like your sister. I must say, though, that it's hard to believe you *are* sisters."

Well, thanks a lot. I've heard that plenty of times, but it never gets any easier. Most people say it when they find out what a dud I am in school. (I can barely *spell*.) I think this teacher meant, though, that Janine and I don't look alike. We *certainly* don't dress alike. For instance, that day, Janine was wearing one of her usual plain outfits—a long pleated plaid skirt, a white shirt with a round collar, stockings, and blue heels. Her hair is short and cut in a pageboy style, so she can't do much with it. I, on the other hand, was dressed in one of my usual wild outfits—a very short black skirt, an over-sized white shirt with bright pink and turquoise poodles printed on it, flat turquoise shoes with ankle straps, and a ton of jewellery, including dangly poodle earrings. My long hair was swept to one side in a high ponytail held in place with a huge pink hairslide.

People kept looking at Janine and then looking at me. I could tell they were all

9

thinking, I can't believe you're sisters. Then they would ignore me and congratulate Janine.

I couldn't wait to leave that main hall.

2nd CHAPTER

I have never been so relieved as I was when Dad put his hand on my shoulder and said, "Well, Claudia, shall we leave?"

Shall we leave? It was all I'd been thinking about for the last hour. Now the final bell at SHS had rung and most people were filing out of the main hall. The only ones left were a few of the kids who'd received awards, a few parents, a few friends, and Mum and Dad and me. Peaches and Russ were gone.

I wanted to say to Dad, "Oh, thank you, thank you, thank you. I can't wait to get out of here." Instead I said (and believe me, this took plenty of control), "Okay. I think I'm ready."

"Right. Janine's going to come home later. She's going out with friends to celebrate first."

Celebrate where? At the library?

I looked at Janine's friends. (There weren't very many of them.) The boys were carrying slide rules and protractors in their shirt pockets. So were the girls, I realized. And not one of them looked like they'd seen the inside of a clothes shop in years. The boys' trousers were too short, and both girls and boys were wearing things that didn't match, like checks with plaids. How did they dress in the morning? By closing their eyes, reaching into their wardrobes, and wearing whatever they happened to pull out?

I knew my thoughts were very mean. I was just annoyed because of all the attention Janine was getting.

Anyway, Mum and Dad and I said goodbye to my sister, and then we walked outside.

"See you later, sweetie," Mum called to me as she slid into the front seat of her car. "I should be home straight after your club meeting."

"Okay, Mum. 'Bye!"

Dad and I got into his car. I tried not to show how upset I was feeling. I didn't want Dad to think I was jealous. But I was.

Also, it was Monday.

The only good thing about any Monday is that my friends and I hold a Babysitters Club meeting after school. We hold meetings on Wednesday and Friday afternoons, too. The club, which is really a business, was started by my friend Kristy Thomas to babysit for kids in our neighbourhoods. I like the club for two reasons. One, I love babysitting. Two, I love having a group of close friends. In fact, I should probably introduce you to my friends.

The club members are Kristy Thomas, Stacey McGill (she's my best friend), Mary Anne Spier, Dawn Schafer, Mallory Pike, Jessi Ramsey, and me (of course). Oh, there are also two associate members who don't come to meetings—their names are Shannon Kilbourne and Logan Bruno (a boy!)—but I'll explain about them later.

Let me introduce you first to Kristy, since she's the chairman and founder of the Babysitters Club (or BSC). Kristy has quite a family! Mine seems so ordinary compared to hers. Kristy used to live opposite me. In fact, she and I and Mary Anne Spier (who also used to live opposite me, next door to Kristy) pretty much grew up together. Kristy has three brothers—two older ones, Sam and Charlie, who go to SHS with Janine—and a little one, David Michael, who's seven. Soon after David Michael was born, Mr Thomas walked out on his family, leaving Mrs Thomas to bring up four kids by herself. (Mr Thomas lives in California or somewhere now.) Anyway, Mrs Thomas managed to keep her family together fine. She found a really good job, and Kristy's life fell into a comfortable routine without her father, even though she missed him, of course. Then Mrs Thomas met Watson Brewer, a divorced millionaire with two small children—and Kristy's whole life changed. Her mother married Watson, and the Thomas family moved into the Brewer mansion on the other side of town. Kristy had suddenly acquired a stepfather, a stepbrother (Andrew, who's four), and a step-sister (Karen, who's just turned seven). Even though Andrew and Karen live with their mother most of the time and only stay with Watson every other weekend, the Thomas/Brewer household is sort of chaotic. First of all, the Brewers adopted a two-year-old Vietnamese girl—Emily Michelle—not long ago, and when that happened, Nannie, Kristy's grandmother, moved in to look after Emily while Mr and Mrs Brewer are at work. Second, there are two other (non-human) members of the household. They are Shannon, David Michael's puppy, and Boo-Boo, Watson's fat old cat.

What kind of person is Kristy? Well, she's strong. She'd have to be to have survived all the changes she's been through. She's also responsible, outgoing, and out-spoken. I suppose *outspoken* is a polite way to describe her. Actually, she has a big mouth and she tends to speak without thinking first, although she never means to be rude. She just says what's on her mind. Kristy is also a tomboy and coaches a softball team for little kids here in Stoney-brook. Her team is called Kristy's Krushers. I guess one of the most important things about Kristy is that she's an ideas person. She is always getting good ideas—and carrying them out. That's one reason she's the chairman of our club.

Kristy has brown hair, brown eyes, and is the shortest kid in our class. I have a feeling she doesn't think she's pretty, but she is. She'd look even better if she took some interest in her clothes, but Kristy wears practically the same outfit day in and day out—jeans, a plain shirt, running shoes, and if the weather is cold, a sweater. Sometimes she wears her Krushers T-shirt instead of the shirt, and often she wears a baseball cap with a collie on it. (The Thomases used to have a collie, Louie, but he died, which is why they got Shannon.)

Kristy's best friend is Mary Anne Spier. It's funny, but Kristy and Mary Anne actually look a little alike. Mary Anne also has brown hair and brown eyes, and she's on the small side, but there the similarities end. I suppose best friends can be opposites and it doesn't matter. While Kristy is outgoing, Mary Anne is shy and quiet, especially with people she doesn't know well. She's also very sensitive (she cries at everything—don't ever see a sad film with her), and she's a good listener, someone to go to with a problem. Also, she's romantic, so I suppose it's fitting that Mary Anne, even though she's shy, is the first of us BSC members to have a steady boyfriend. Guess who he is? Logan Bruno, one of our associate members!

Like Kristy, Mary Anne's got an interesting family—but it's very different from Kristy's. For starters, Mrs Spier died when Mary Anne was very little so, Mary Anne grew up in quite a lonely atmosphere. It was just her and her father for a long time, and Mr Spier was really strict, trying to bring up his only child by himself. He made up all these rules for Mary Anne, including rules about how she could dress. But about a year ago, when he saw how mature and responsible Mary Anne really is, he started to loosen up. Now Mary Anne dresses in pretty trendy clothes instead of the Janine-like way her father made her dress, although she still isn't allowed to get her ears pierced, use much make-up, or put on any nail-varnish other than clear.

A little while ago, Mr Spier began to loosen up even more. That was because he began dating again—and he was dating the mother of Dawn Schafer, another BSC member! You see, a *long* time ago Mrs Schafer and Mr Spier had gone to Stoneybrook High School together. Then Mrs Schafer (who was Sharon Porter at the time) went off to college in California, where she met and married Mr Schafer. Together they had Dawn and her younger brother, Jeff, before they got divorced. After the divorce, Mrs Schafer moved back to Stoneybrook, her hometown, with Dawn and Jeff. Dawn and Mary Anne became best friends (Mary Anne has two best friends), and then Mrs Schafer remet Mr Spier, they began going out together again, and finally . . . they got married! So now Mary Anne and Dawn are best friends, club members, *and* stepsisters. As far as Mary Anne is concerned, the only bad thing about all this is that she, her father, and her kitten, Tigger, had to move out of the house in which Mary Anne had grown up, and into Dawn's house because it's bigger. But she's getting used to things.

I should probably tell you about Dawn next, since you already know a little about her. Dawn is our California girl. Having grown up out there, she likes (and misses) the hot weather and sunshine, and had a hard time adjusting to our Connecticut winters. Dawn also likes health food (her whole family does), and would rather eat tofu and broccoli than an ice-cream sundae. And she loves ghost stories and haunted houses and mysteries, which is pretty interesting considering that the colonial farmhouse she moved into in Stoneybrook has an actual secret passage (one end of it is in Dawn's *bedroom*), and there's a good chance that the house, or at least the passage, is haunted.

If Kristy and Mary Anne are on the

pretty side, then Dawn is out-and-out gorgeous. Her hair is incredibly long and incredibly blonde (it's practically white), and her eyes are a piercing blue. She's slim, and a terrific dresser, although her style is different from that of any other BSC member. We call it California casual—loose clothes, bright colours, trendy but not outrageous. Dawn is an individual and pretty much does what she pleases (without hurting anyone's feelings). Her clothes are unique, she's got two holes pierced in each ear, and she doesn't care (much) what other people think of her. She just sort of goes her own way. I tend to think of Dawn as strong, like Kristy, but one thing really tore her apart. That was when her brother, Jeff, moved *back* to California to live with their father. He'd never been happy in Connecticut, had never adjusted like Dawn had. Dawn knew it was the right thing for him, but she misses him a lot, and now her family is broken in two and separated by three thousand miles. She does like having a stepfather, though, and she especially likes her stepsister, so things have been better for Dawn lately.

My best friend in the whole world is Stacey McGill. Stacey is an only child who grew up in big, exciting New York City. But she and her parents moved to Stoneybrook at the beginning of the seventh grade because the company her father works for transferred him to Connecticut. Stacey and I became best friends very quickly. She was my first best friend! But she had only been here for a year when her father was transferred *back* to New York. I was almost as sad then as I was when Mimi died. However, the McGills had been in New York again for less than a year when Stacey's parents decided to get a divorce—and Mrs McGill decided to move back to Stoneybrook, which she had loved. Stacey was allowed to choose whether to live here with her mother or in New York with her father, and she finally settled on Stoneybrook. I'm so glad to have Stacey back, even though I'm *really* sorry about the reason she's here. I know she misses her father terribly, even though she's allowed to visit him any time she wants (except on school days). She hated having to choose between her parents.

As best friends, Stacey and I are much more alike than Kristy and Mary Anne or Dawn and Mary Anne are. We're both sophisticated and mature for thirteen (I suppose that sounds a little stuck-up, but I really think it's true), and we're both *very* into clothes and style. We have pierced ears (Stacey has a hole in each ear, and I have one hole in one ear and two in the other), we're both wild dressers, and Stacey even gets to perm her blonde hair every now and then. Stacey's always trying out new things like painting designs on her nails or putting glitter in her hair.

Stacey is funny, sweet, and a much better pupil than I am. In maths, she's nearly a genius, although I hate to use that word. But she has one problem. She's diabetic. This doesn't bother any of us club members, of course, but it does *worry* us sometimes. Stacey has got awfully thin lately, she has to give herself daily injections of something called insulin, and she has to stay on a strict, and I mean *strict*, diet. You see, diabetes is a disease in which an organ called the pancreas doesn't make enough of a hormone, insulin, to control the blood sugar in someone's body. (Ugh! biology.) So without the injections and the no-sweets diet to control her blood sugar, Stacey could get really ill. She could even go into a coma. Stacey knows this, so she tries hard to do what her doctors tell her, but in all honesty, there are some days when she just doesn't feel too good. Stacey copes, though.

Before I tell you about the last two club members, Jessi Ramsey and Mallory Pike, let me finish telling you about me. You've already heard about my family, my art, how I feel about school, and how I'm like Stacey. Here are just two more things about me: 1. I *love* junk food and keep tons of it in my room. 2. Although I don't really like to read, I do like Nancy Drew mysteries. But I have to keep both the junk food and the mysteries hidden, because my parents don't approve of either one. They don't approve of the

20

junk food for obvious reasons, and they don't approve of Nancy Drew because they think I should be reading "literature". Mimi used to say, "I don't care what you read, my Claudia, as long as you read." I like her way of thinking better than Mum and Dad's. Anyway, my room can be a surprising place. When you open a drawer or turn over a pillow, you never know if you're going to find a hidden packet of Maltesers or maybe a copy of *Mystery at the Moss-Covered Mansion*.

Okay. On to Jessi and Mal. The first thing to know about them is that they're the younger members of the BSC. While Kristy, Stacey, Mary Anne, Dawn, and I are in the eighth grade, they're in the sixth. They're also best friends with a lot of similarities and a lot of differences. For instance, each of them is the oldest one in her family, and they both feel that their parents treat them like babies. Eleven is a hard age, I suppose. I wouldn't want to be eleven again. I remember that my mother expected me to be mature then, but also wouldn't give me many privileges. However, Jessi's and Mal's parents *did* let them get their ears pierced recently. (Kristy and Mary Anne are the only club members who don't have pierced ears.) But now Mal's got a brace on her teeth, and she wears glasses and isn't allowed to get contact lenses yet, and neither Mal nor Jessi is allowed to babysit at night, so they still have a long way to go.

Both Jessi and Mallory have younger brothers and sisters, but Jessi has just two— her eight-year-old sister, Becca, and her baby brother, who's nicknamed Squirt— while Mal has *seven*. And three of her brothers are identical triplets! Also, both girls like to read, especially horse stories, but Jessi's other interest is ballet, while Mal likes writing and drawing. Jessi is a really talented ballerina. You should see her dance. She goes to special classes at a ballet school in Stamford, and she has performed leading roles on stage in front of lots of people. Mallory is talented, too. She keeps a journal, and is always writing and illustrating stories. She says she wants to be an author and illustrator of children's books one day.

One last difference between the girls. Mal is white and Jessi is black. I don't see what the big deal is, but when the Ramseys first moved to Stoneybrook (and by the way, they bought Stacey's house when the McGills went back to New York!), people here gave Jessi's family a really hard time. Some people wouldn't let their kids play with Becca, other people just avoided the Ramseys. I suppose this is because there aren't many black families in Stoneybrook (Jessi's the only black student in the whole of the sixth grade), but *honestly*, what's wrong with people? At least things have quietened down. Becca and Jessi have got friends now, and most of the Ramseys' neighbours have accepted them, thank goodness.

So those are my friends, the ones I'd see in just a few hours when our first BSC meeting of the week got underway.

3rd CHAPTER

I felt as if I'd been watching clocks all day. First I'd watched the one in the science lesson. Now I was in my room watching my own clock as the digital numbers flipped towards five-thirty. I was waiting for our BSC meeting to begin. The meetings are always held in my room, the official club headquarters.

While I waited for my friends to arrive, I started thinking about the BSC, so I'll tell you about our club, how it got started, and how it works. As I said earlier, Kristy is the chairman and founder of the club. It was one of her big ideas. She got the idea back at the beginning of the seventh grade. In those days, she (and Mary Anne) still lived across the street from me, and Watson Brewer hadn't yet proposed to Kristy's mother. Mrs Thomas was working full-time, and David Michael was just six then, so it was up to Kristy, Sam, and Charlie to take turns looking after him in the afternoons. This arrangement was fine until the day came when nobody—not Kristy, or one of her brothers—was free to sit for David Michael. So Mrs Thomas started phoning baby-sitters. Since it was a last-minute situation, she had to make call after call, trying to find someone who wasn't already busy. Kristy watched her mother doing this and thought it would be great if a parent could make one call and reach a whole group of babysitters at once, instead of having to make so many individual calls? And that's how her great idea was born. She discussed it with Mary Anne and me, since all three of us did some babysitting, and then she asked us to form a babysitting club with her. Of course, we agreed straight away, but we decided that three people weren't enough. I suggested that we invite Stacey McGill to join the club, too. She had only just moved here, but she and I were already getting to be good friends. Stacey was glad to join the club. She had babysat in New York, and she wanted to meet people in Stoneybrook.

So that was the beginning of the club. We decided to hold our meetings three times a week, on Monday, Wednesday, and Friday afternoons from five-thirty until six. Parents could phone us at those times and they would reach *four* experienced sitters at once. They were bound to get a sitter with just one phone call.

How did people know about our club and when to phone us? We advertised. We sent out dozens of leaflets in our neighbourhoods, and we even placed an advert in the *Stoneybrook News*. Sure enough, we got job calls at our first meeting, and business has just got better and better ever since. By the middle of the seventh grade, we even needed a new member to help us out, so we asked Dawn (who had just moved here) to join the club. Then when (gulp) Stacey moved away, we replaced her with both Jessi and Mal, but naturally we let Stacey back into the club when she returned to Stoneybrook. Now we have seven members and two associate members, and Kristy says the BSC is big enough.

We run our club very officially and professionally, thanks mostly to Kristy. Kristy makes us keep a notebook in which we write about every job we take. Then we're responsible for reading the book once a week. None of us really likes doing this, but we have to admit that knowing what's going on with the families we sit for and seeing how our friends solve sitting problems is pretty helpful.

Also, each of us holds a certain position in the club. Kristy is the chairman, since she started the club, and since she has such great ideas for it. One of her great ideas was

26

Kid-Kits. A Kid-Kit is a decorated box (we each have one) filled with our old toys, books, and games, as well as new items such as colouring books and art supplies, that we sometimes take with us on babysitting jobs. Kids love them—which makes us popular sitters and really helps our business!

I'm the vice-chairman. This is mostly because I have a phone in my room and my own private phone number. We can take calls here without tying up someone else's line or getting a lot of calls that aren't for us. That's why my room is club headquarters.

Our secretary is Mary Anne. She probably has the biggest job of any of us. It's up to her to keep the club book in order. The record book (which is entirely different from the notebook) is where we keep track of all important club information: the names and addresses of our clients, the money we earn and how our club subs are spent (that's really Stacey's job—she's the treasurer), and our schedules and appointments for babysitting jobs. Scheduling is the biggest of Mary Anne's duties and she's really good at it. This is lucky, since originally we just wanted Mary Anne to be the secretary because she had the nicest handwriting of all of us. We had no idea what her job would turn into. Mary Anne has to keep track of my art classes, Jessi's ballet lessons, Mal's orthodontist appointments, etc., in addition to scheduling every job that's called in.

Mary Anne is terrific at this. As far as we know, she has not made one mistake. We're grateful to her for that.

As I mentioned before, Stacey is the club treasurer. It's her job to record the money we earn. This is just for our own interest. Each member gets to keep all the money she earns on a job. We don't try to divide the money up or anything. Stacey is also in charge of collecting our weekly subs each Monday. She loves this part of her job. Stacey likes having money (even when it's club money, not her own), and hates parting with it. But she does have to part with it. The subs money goes into the club treasury (a manila envelope) and is spent on various things: paying Charlie to drive Kristy back and forth to BSC meetings now that she lives so far from my neighbourhood, paying part of my monthly phone bill, buying items—such as art supplies, soap bubbles, or activity books—for the Kid-Kits, and . . . fun things! We like to have a club sleepover or pizza party every now and then. Since Stacey is so great at maths, she makes a very good treasurer.

Dawn is the club's alternate officer. That means that she can take over the job of anyone who can't make a meeting. For instance, if Mary Anne were ill, Dawn could handle the notebook and do the scheduling until Mary Anne felt better. Dawn is like a substitute teacher (except that we don't throw spitballs behind her back when she's in charge). In case you're wondering, Dawn became the treasurer when Stacey moved back to New York, but she gladly handed the job over to Stace again when she returned. Dawn is a good pupil, but she's not as quick at maths as Stacey is. Besides, she hated collecting subs because we're all so crabby about parting with even a little of our hard-earned money. At one time or another, Dawn has taken over every job except Kristy's. Guess why? Our chairman has never missed a meeting.

Jessi and Mallory are the club's junior officers. They don't have actual jobs, though. *Junior officer* means that they aren't allowed to babysit at night (unless they're sitting for their own brothers and sisters). They can only sit after school and at weekends. This is still a big help. The junior officers free us older members for evening jobs.

Last but not least, our club has the two associate members I mentioned earlier— Shannon Kilbourne and Logan Bruno. Shannon is a friend of Kristy's. She lives across the street from Kristy in her new neighbourhood, and she goes to a private school, so nobody but Kristy sees her very often. Logan, as I've mentioned, is Mary Anne's boyfriend. He's an eighth-grader at SMS with us, and he is sooooo nice. He's perfect for Mary Anne. He's funny, sweet, and understands Mary Anne and her moods really well. Logan's family comes from Louisville, Kentucky, and Logan speaks with this terrific southern accent. Anyway, both Logan and Shannon have done a lot of babysitting, so as associate members, they're our backups. They're people we can call on just in case the BSC is offered a job that none of us can take. Believe it or not, that *does* happen sometimes. And when it does, we like to be able to say, "We're sorry, none of us can take the job, but let us recommend one of our associate members." Then we phone Logan or Shannon—and we don't have to disappoint our client.

I think that's everything you need to know about the BSC. It may sound complicated, but it really isn't. And belonging to the club is great fun. That's why I couldn't wait for my friends to arrive on that bleak Monday when Janine had won her ten millionth award and I'd got left in the dust again.

At 5:20, Kristy arrived. At 5:23, Dawn and Mary Anne arrived. And by 5:29, we had all gathered in my room and taken our usual places. Kristy sat herself in my director's chair, wearing a visor, a pencil stuck over one ear. Mallory and Jessi sat on the floor, leaning against my bed. Dawn and Mary Anne and I lined ourselves up on my bed, leaning against the wall, and Stacey sat backwards in my desk chair, facing into the room, her arms slung over the top rung of the back. (Sometimes Dawn sits in the desk chair and Stacey joins Mary Anne and me on the bed.)

As soon as my digital clock turned from 5:29 to 5:30, Kristy (who'd been watching that clock like a hawk) said, "Order! Come to order, please!"

The rest of us stopped talking. Mal and Jessi put down the paper chain they've been making out of chewing gum wrappers since the beginning of time.

And before Kristy had even finished saying, "Any club business?" Stacey had leapt up, grabbed the club treasury, and was passing it round, saying, "Subs day! Subs day! Fork out, everyone!"

With sighs and groans, my friends and I reached into pockets or purses, pulled out our subs, and dropped them in the manila envelope. Then Stacey plopped onto the floor, emptied out all the money, counted it up in her head just by looking at it, and announced, "We're rich!"

She parcelled out money to Kristy, who needed to pay Charlie, and to Dawn, Jessi, and Mary Anne, who needed new items for their Kid-Kits. Just as she was finishing, the phone began ringing. Mary Anne scheduled four jobs. As soon as she had finished (and as soon as I'd handed round a bag of marshmallows, which everyone except Stacey and Dawn helped themselves

31

to), Kristy said, "I have some business to discuss." She adjusted her visor. "Well, it's not exactly business, but you should know what's going on with Emily Michelle at the moment." (We try to keep each other informed about problems with kids the club sits for.)

"With Emily?" Mary Anne repeated. "Is something wrong? Is it serious?" (Mary Anne gets worked up very easily.)

"I—I don't know. I mean no, well . . . yes." Kristy drew in a breath. "Okay. This is it. You know how Doctor Dellenkamp says Emily is language-delayed?"

The rest of us nodded. We knew, and it made sense. Emily had grown up in Vietnam, where the people around her spoke a different language. And part of her life had been spent in an orphanage, where she probably didn't get a lot of attention. So it was no wonder that at two, she didn't speak much English.

"Well," Kristy went on, "the paediatrician says Emily isn't making as much progress as she'd expected. Also, Emily has some emotional problems. She's started having these nightmares—at least, we think she's having nightmares—and she wakes up screaming 'Me! Me!'" (Kristy pronounced the word as if she were saying "met", but leaving the "t" off the end.) "'Me'," she informed us, "is what Vietnamese children say for 'Mama' or 'Mummy'. Also she

32

seems scared of everything—the dark, loud noises, trying new things, and being separated from any of us, especially Mum and Watson. Doctor Dellenkamp isn't too worried about the fears, even though Mum and Watson are. The doctor says the fears are a delayed reaction to all the upheaval in Emily's life. You know, losing her mother, going to the orphanage, getting adopted, moving to a new country. The doctor says Emily will outgrow the fears and nightmares. She's more worried about Emily's speech, and even how she *plays*. She says she doesn't play like a two-year-old yet. She still thinks Emily will catch up, though."

Kristy sighed. "I wish", she continued, "that I could spend more time with Emily, but I've got that job at the Papadakises' now."

The Papadakises live across the street and one house down from Kristy. They have three kids. The oldest is a boy, Linny, who's friends with David Michael. Then there's seven-year-old Hannie, who's one of Karen's best friends, and Sari, who's about Emily's age. Recently, their grandfather fell and broke his hip, so he had to go into a nursing home to recover. While he was there, he came down with pneumonia, and he's pretty ill. Of course, Mr and Mrs Papadakis want to be with him as much as possible, so they've asked Kristy to sit for them three evenings a week, plus some in-between times. (I think they've signed up other sitters, too. Shannon Kilbourne, for one.)

We were all saying things like, "Gosh, Kristy, that's too bad," and, "Try not to worry *too* much," when the phone rang again.

Jessi answered it. "Hi, Mrs Brewer!" she said brightly. (It was Kristy's mum!) She listened for a moment. Then she said, "Okay, we'll check the schedule and get right back to you." Jessi put the phone down. "Your mum needs a sitter for next Friday night," she said. "She knows you'll be at the Papadakises' then. She says she needs someone for about three hours to watch David Michael and Emily Michelle. Andrew and Karen won't be there that weekend."

Mary Anne checked the record book. "Claud," she said, "you're free that night. Want the job?"

"Of course!" I replied.

I was beginning to feel a little more cheerful. I'd almost forgotten about the awards ceremony that afternoon.

4th CHAPTER

My good mood didn't last long. As soon as the meeting was over and my friends had left, I began to feel a bit depressed. I flopped down on my bed and propped my leg up on a pillow. I broke that leg not long ago, and now, every time it's going to rain, my legs aches.

Goody, I thought sarcastically. Rain. That'll improve my mood.

I lay there and went over the events of the day. Monday had started out with Janine coming into my room about fifty times, each time in a different outfit—although her clothes are so boring that the outfits all looked the same to me.

I don't like any of Janine's clothes, so I told her each outfit looked fine, which confused her. She chose the dull awards-ceremony outfit by herself.

Then there was breakfast, during which

all Mum and Dad talked about were the logistics (what *are* "logistics"?) of leaving work early, picking me up, and getting to the high school on time.

In maths class that day we got a test back. What was my grade? A C-, that's what.

Janine does as well with maths as she does with computers and science.

Finally, there had been the stupid ceremony, and we all know how that went.

"Claudia! . . . Claudia?"

My mother was calling to me from downstairs. I was supposed to be helping with dinner. It was my turn.

"Coming!" I called back. And I limped downstairs, where I made an absolutely gorgeous salad to go with supper. I made radish roses, and arranged carrot sticks and slices of hard-boiled eggs to look like the sun. It was a work of art. It was a culinary masterpiece. (I know what "culinary" means, believe it or not. It means "having to do with cooking".)

Wouldn't you know? When my family had gathered for dinner and I had put the salad on the table, Dad said, "Claudia, how lovely! A celebratory salad for Janine!"

Celebratory salad my foot. I'd just been having fun being creative.

I tried not to act upset, though. I sat down at my place and smiled a fake smile.

Guess what? The very second we'd all been served, Dad said (with this big grin on his face), "Well, that was some ceremony this afternoon, Janine. Your mother and sister and I certainly are proud of you."

Janine pretended to be embarrassed, but she couldn't fool me. I knew she was loving every bit of the attention she was getting. "Thanks," she said, ducking her head.

"Well?" Dad went on. "Do you want to surprise your sister and your mother with the other news?"

Other news? There was *more*? This wasn't over yet?

"All right," said Janine. She put her fork down and wiped her mouth daintily. "After you left the high school today, a reporter from one of the Stamford papers arrived. She wants to interview me. And the college paper does, too. They even want to follow me around and photograph me at SHS and at home. They want to portray what the writer called 'A Day in the Life of a Genius'."

Oh, please. Give me a break.

I couldn't stand it. I crammed four slices of hard-boiled egg into my mouth. I did that so that if Janine said, "What do you think, Claudia? Do you want to be in the article?" I wouldn't be able to answer her. At least, not until I'd swallowed, and that would take a while.

But she didn't say anything. The subject changed—to Janine's cheque.

"What are you going to do with the

money, darling?" asked Mum. "It's yours. You can do whatever you want with it."

It was *hers*? Wow! If I were handed a cheque for $250, I'd run to Bellair's Department Store and buy the Day-Glo green sweater with charms knitted into it that I'd seen in the sale. Then I'd go to the art shop and buy some new oil paints, a good supply of brushes, and the great silk-screening set I've had my eye on. After that, if any money was left over, I'd hit the sweet shop in a big way. Mmm—Dime Bars, Maltesers, M&Ms (plain and peanut); Mintolas . . . Oh, the possibilities were endless. Janine was *so lucky*.

"I think," said my sister slowly, "that I'll put the money towards college."

All of it? That was the most boring thing I'd heard in years. I could almost hear her idea fall to the floor. *Clunk*.

Of course, Mum and Dad grinned with pride.

I felt invisible. Nobody had said anything to me since that comment about the celebratory salad. I wished desperately that Mimi were alive. If she were, she'd have been sitting right next to me. And she would have known how I was feeling. She'd have shared in Janine's triumph, but then she would have said to me, "Tell me, my Claudia, how was your club meeting today? Did you get any babysitting jobs?" Mimi always knew the right thing to say.

At last, dinner was over. As we were clearing the table, I thought, hurray, I've survived. Now I can escape and—

But Mum pulled me aside and whispered, "We have a surprise for Janine. A cake! Make sure she stays in the dining room while I get it ready."

So we had to eat this bakery cake that was covered with yellow roses and said CON-GRATULATIONS, JEANINE in blue icing. The best part about the cake was that someone had spelt my sister's name wrong.

Finally dinner was *really* over. I had intended to do my homework, but I knew I wouldn't be able to concentrate, not with Janine's computer clicking away in her room. Every tap on the keyboard would remind me of her award and how clever she was and how stupid I was. So I wandered into our study for some peace and quiet.

At first I just sat in the armchair and stared round the room. After a while, my eyes rested on our family photo albums that were lined up in the bookcase. I took the oldest ones down and began to leaf through them. The first one was mostly pictures of Mum and Dad during the first couple of years after they'd got married. The second one was full of Janine's baby pictures. I'd never noticed it before, but honestly, there were an awful *lot* of pictures of Janine. There were pictures of her being held by every relative we had; pictures of her

wearing funny hats, wearing a big pair of
sunglasses, looking at a magazine (she was
probably *reading* it); pictures of her at her
first, second, and third birthday parties, and
even a picture of Mum and Dad holding
Janine in front of the hospital the day they'd
brought her home. Who had taken that
picture? Mimi? Peaches? A nurse?

With a sigh, I closed the album, put it
down, and picked up the next one. This, I
thought, must be full of pictures of me.

But it wasn't. Not exactly. It was full of
pictures of Janine and me. There I was in
Janine's lap. I was just a baby. My head was
falling back and Janine was crying. There I
was in Janine's lap again as she tried to give
me a bottle. There we were when I was older
and Janine was helping me to walk. Then I
found a whole load of pictures of Janine's
fourth birthday party.

So where were the pictures of *me*? I
turned to the beginning of the album to see
if I'd missed anything—like a picture of
Mum and Dad bringing me home from the
hospital. I hadn't missed a thing.

I began looking at the pictures of Janine
and me again. I looked at them carefully.
We don't look a bit alike now, but maybe
we'd looked alike when we were little, when
our parents dressed us in matching clothes
and gave us the same haircuts.

Nope. We barely looked related.

When I thought about it, not only do I

not look like Janine, I don't look like my parents, either, although Janine looks exactly like Dad.

A funny feeling crept into my stomach. I replaced the photo albums on the shelves. Then I silently pushed the door to the study until it was almost closed, tiptoed to my parents' desk, and began looking through the drawers. I felt like a thief, but I was just hoping to find more photos. Mum and Dad, I decided, must have taken several rolls of pictures of me as a baby and simply not had time to put them in any albums. I wanted to find those pictures badly. I especially wanted to find at least one of me coming home from the hospital.

Nothing.

I found paper clips and rubber bands, scissors and glue, enough pens and pencils for an army, an envelope containing Janine's and my report cards (I put that away quickly), a packet of letters and cards from Peaches, Russ, and other relatives, a certificate that said that Mum was certified to teach in elementary schools in the state of Connecticut (*that* was a surprise), some bank books, some boring-looking files, and then . . . right at the back of the bottom drawer . . . I found a locked cash box. That was weird. Where was the key? I searched the desk, but the only keys I found were spare house keys.

What was in that box?

All of a sudden it dawned on me. I knew. I just *knew*. I was *adopted*, and my adoption papers were in there. If I was adopted, that would explain why I didn't look like anyone in my family, why I didn't *act* like anyone in my family, and why there were so few pictures of me. I wasn't Mum and Dad's *real* child. I was an unwanted baby, or an orphan like Emily Michelle.

I wished again for Mimi. If Mimi were here I would go straight to her and say, "Am I adopted?" and she would give me an honest answer. But Mimi was gone. And there was no way I was going to ask Mum and Dad that question. They'd probably say I was just feeling grumpy because Janine had got so much attention that day.

I straightened up the desk, making sure it looked as it had before I'd begun searching through it. Then I swung open the door to the study and went upstairs to my room. I sat at my own desk and thought, am I really adopted? Who are my real mother and father? Why did they give me away? . . . *Who am I?*

5th CHAPTER

All week I kept the awful secret of my adoption to myself. I didn't even tell Stacey what I'd discovered, and Stacey is my best friend in the world. I *wanted* to talk to Stacey but I couldn't. Not yet. There must, I thought, be some terrible reason for keeping my adoption a secret. But what could the terrible reason be? Whatever it was, it wasn't *my* fault. A *baby* couldn't do anything wrong. Maybe someone had stolen me from a hospital and sold me to a crooked lawyer who had let Mum and Dad (the people I thought were my real parents) adopt me for a huge sum of money. Then Mum and Dad took me home, but later they found out that I was stolen, only they were afraid to return me. Maybe we all had different identities now. We were incognito and in hiding.

Nah. I'd been watching too many films lately.

Still, if I was adopted, I wanted to know about it.

On Friday night I babysat for David Michael and Emily Michelle at Kristy's mansion. They're both good kids, but it turned out to be a tough sitting job. David Michael was recovering from a cold, so he was crabby and didn't feel well, and Kristy wasn't kidding when she said Emily was having some problems. I got to see the problems for myself.

I reached the Brewer/Thomas mansion at five minutes to seven. (Dad dropped me off. Kristy's mum would drive me home later.) As I walked to the front door, I could hear the low rumble of distant thunder. I glanced up. The sky looked threatening. And the wind was beginning to blow. We're in for a storm, I thought.

I rang the bell as Dad pulled into the street. Kristy answered the door. She was on her way over to the Papadakises'.

"Hello and goodbye!" she said cheerfully. "You know where I'll be if you have any problems."

"Okay," I said. "See you later."

Kristy ran outside, then ran back in, grabbed an umbrella from a stand in the hallway, saying, "It feels like it's going to pour!" and left again.

44

"Hi, Claudia!" called Mrs Brewer. "It's nice to see you! How are you?" (I don't get over to Kristy's house very often. I used to see Mrs Brewer nearly every day.)

"I'm fine," I replied. What else could I say? I'm adopted, thank you, how are you? No way.

"That's good. Now let's see," Mrs Brewer began. "Sam and Charlie have gone to see a play at the high school. They've just left. You know where Kristy is, my mother has gone out to dinner with some of her friends, and Mr Brewer and I will be at the Morgans', down the street. We should all be home by about nine-thirty. The Morgans' and the Papadakises' numbers are in the kitchen with the emergency numbers. I'm sorry to say that I'm leaving you with a couple of problems. David Michael is upstairs in bed. He's had a cold for several days, and he's on the mend, but he isn't feeling too well. Has Kristy told you about Emily Michelle?"

"Yes," I said.

"Okay. Expect a few tears when Mr Brewer and I leave, and you might have a little trouble getting her to sleep, but Emily knows you, so she should be all right. Now, bedtimes are . . ."

Kristy's mum gave me a few more instructions, and then she and Watson (I always think of Kristy's stepfather as

"Watson" because that's what Kristy calls him) started to put on their coats.

"'Bye!" they called upstairs to David Michael. "Sleep well. Feel better. We'll see you tomorrow morning!"

"'Bye," David Michael replied weakly.

I stood in the hallway, holding Emily, who watched her parents put on their coats. No sooner did Watson reach for the door, than Emily let out a loud wail.

"No bye-bye!" she cried. She held her arms out, straining toward Kristy's mother.

The Brewers were pretty cool about this. They just kissed Emily, called "Goodbye!" very cheerfully, and slipped out of the door.

I suppose a quick exit is best—but I was left with a screaming child. Emily was still yelling, "No bye-bye!" She began to struggle, so I put her down. Emily ran to the door and threw herself at it in tears.

Well, that was no good.

"Come on, Miss Emily," I said. "Let's go upstairs and see how David Michael's doing. You're not alone here, you know. Do you want to see your brother?"

Emily's reply was another wail, so I picked her up again and carried her up to David Michael's room. By the time we reached it, she was whimpering, but not really crying.

"Hiya, David Michael," I said. "How are you feeling?"

"Fide," he replied stuffily, but he certainly

didn't sound fine. He didn't look fine, either. In fact, he looked pretty cross. "What's wrong with *her*?" he asked, pointing to Emily.

"Emily's upset because your parents have just left," I answered.

"Oh." David Michael, who was propped up in bed, a portable TV on and the remote control within easy reach, turned back to a comic he'd been looking at.

"Buh!" said Emily, whose tears were drying. I set her on the floor and she made a beeline for the remote control.

David Michael held it above his head.

"BUH!" cried Emily, grabbing for it.

"Can't Emily play with that?" I asked David Michael.

"Doe," he replied. "She breaks theb. She presses all the buttuds at the sabe tibe. She's dot allowed."

"Okay," I said. "Listen, David Michael, I'm going to give Emily a bath. Do you need anything?"

"Just sub orange juice."

So I got David Michael a glass of orange juice, and gave Emily a bath. The bath was surprisingly easy. At least Emily wasn't afraid of water.

When Emily was dried off and in her nightdress, I took her back to David Michael's room. "Bedtime," I told him. "For both you and Emily. Your mum said you have to go to sleep early because of your cold. Do you need anything else?"

"Cad you put the Kleenex dearer to by bed? I bight deed theb id the biddle of the dight."

I moved the Kleenex. "Anything else?"

"Sub water. Ad a wet flannel for by head. Bubby" (Mummy) "said that will bake by dose feel better."

When David Michael was finally settled, I turned out his light, closed the door to his room, and led Emily down the landing.

"Okay. Nighty-night," I told her. I laid her in her cot.

I turned out the light.

"Wah!"

I turned the light back on.

Emily stood up. "Hi!" she said.

Uh-oh. What do I do now? I wondered. Emily *won't* fall asleep with the light off and she *can't* fall asleep with it on. Finally, I went into Karen's room, unplugged her night-light, moved it into Emily's room, turned it on, said "Goodnight," and tiptoed out, leaving the door open a crack so that Emily could see the light in the hallway.

Emily whimpered, but didn't cry. I waited outside her room to make sure she was okay. When a few quiet moments had gone by, I headed for the stairs.

KER-RASH! Thunder.

"Wahhh!"

Drat. The storm had arrived. Emily was

48

terrified. I ran back to her room, picked her up, sat in the rocking chair with her, and just held her until she fell asleep—out of pure exhaustion. Once she was asleep, I was afraid to move. I didn't want to wake her up. But I couldn't sit there with her all night.

Very carefully, I got to my feet. Emily stirred, but she didn't wake up. Whew! I laid her back in her cot. She was still sound asleep.

I crept downstairs.

I had brought my schoolbooks along with me, and I'd fully intended to start my weekend homework, but I couldn't concentrate. All I could think about was Emily—and how she'd been adopted. Emily was lucky. Okay, she was having a few problems, but every day, her mother and father told her about her adoption, even though she was too little to understand. I knew this because Kristy had told me. Every day, Watson or Mrs Brewer would say to Emily that she wasn't just adopted, she was *chosen*. And she was very, very special.

I wished Mum and Dad had told me that so I wouldn't have had to find out on my own when I was thirteen and completely shocked by the news.

Ring, ring!

I dashed into the kitchen and picked up the phone. "Hello, Brewer residence," I said professionally.

"Hi. This is the McGill residence."

"Oh, hi, Stace! What's up?"

"I thought the storm might be scaring you. I've sat at that huge house during storms and it can be terrifying. Are you okay?"

"I suppose so."

"You suppose so? Claud, is anything wrong? You've been quiet all week."

Suddenly I couldn't think of anything I wanted to do more than blurt out my terrible secret to my best friend.

So I did. I told Stacey everything, finishing up with, "I just don't understand why Mum and Dad—and, by the way, they aren't my real parents, you know—why they didn't tell me the truth a long time ago."

"I don't know," said Stacey, disbelievingly. "Claud, are you *sure* you're adopted?"

I started to reply, "Pretty sure," but instead I said, "Positive."

"Then," said Stacey, "I think you should start a search. Look for your real parents. You know you won't feel better until you do."

"You're right," I said slowly.

"Hey!" exclaimed Stace. "There's one good thing about all this."

"What's that?" I asked.

"You and Janine the Genius aren't related!"

I was in the middle of a good laugh when

lightning flashed, thunder sounded, and I heard cries of, "Me! Me! . . . ME!" from upstairs.

"Gotta go," I told Stacey. "The storm has just woken Emily up. I'll talk to you tomorrow. Hey, don't tell anyone about the adoption thing, okay? It's a secret between us."

"Okay," replied Stacey. We got off the phone then and I dashed upstairs to Emily. I held her and rocked her again while she cried and cried. But even as I looked at her tear-stained face, I couldn't help thinking that Emily was luckier than I was. She would never be shocked by the news. And she had *honest* adoptive parents.

6th CHAPTER

Monday

I babysat at your house today, Kristy! You were watching the Papadakis Kids, so I took care of Emily Michelle and David Michael while your grandmother was in a bowling tournament and your parents were at work. Kristy, you know what happened this afternoon since you came over with Linny, Hannie, and Sari, but the rest of you babysitters don't know, so here goes.

The afternoon went fine, basically. David Michael is completely over his cold and back to normal. And Emily was her usual sunny self. There were no thunderstorms or loud noises to scare her, so she

*had a good time while I was
with her, I think. The only
upsetting part was what Kristy
and I talked about....*

Emily *did* have a little trouble when Nannie
left, but not much. Dawn had an easier
babysitting job at Kristy's house than I'd
had. She phoned when she got home afterwards to ask me about some homework, and
we ended up talking about Emily—and
Kristy's fears about Emily.

Dawn and Kristy had caught the bus to
Kristy's house together after school on
Monday. That was the easiest way for Dawn
to get to Kristy's neighbourhood since it's
too far for Dawn (or any of us) to cycle to,
and since both Dawn's mother and stepfather work and couldn't drive her over.

Anyway, when Kristy and Dawn stepped
off the bus, Kristy said, "I'm going straight
to the Papadakises'. Nannie knows that, by
the way. But how about if I bring the kids
over later? David Michael and Linny will be
glad to play, and maybe Emily and Sari
could play, too. Emily doesn't see enough
kids of her own age."

"That'd be great," said Dawn. "Come
round whenever you want." Then she added,
"Hey, I'm inviting you to your own house!"

Kristy laughed, and headed across the
street while Dawn ran up Kristy's drive and
rang the bell.

Nannie answered it. "Hi, Dawn," she said warmly. "Look who's just woken up from her nap."

Nannie was carrying Emily, who was rubbing her eyes. When she saw Dawn, she buried her head in Nannie's neck.

"Little Miss Shy," said Nannie, smiling.

She gave Dawn a few instructions, then handed Emily to her and left as quickly as the Brewers had left on the night I was sitting.

"Good luck in the tournament!" Dawn called after Nannie.

Emily started to wail, but at that moment, David Michael burst through the front door. He had just got off the elementary-school bus.

"Hi, Dawn!" he said. "Hiya, Emily!"

"Day-day," said Emily. Her tears were over before they'd even begun.

"Dawn?" said David Michael after he'd put his things away and had a snack. "Can Timmy come round and play? Timmy Hsu? He lives down the street. He's just moved here. He's a good ballplayer. He wants to join Kristy's Krushers. I said we could play catch so he could practice."

"Of course," replied Dawn. "Give him a call."

So David Michael did, and in no time he and Timmy were throwing a softball around the back garden while Dawn watched Emily. Emily (who's not the world's best walker—

she's on the slow side) toddled over to a flowerbed. She sniffed at a rose. Then she crouched down and poked at a brown leaf. And the next thing Dawn knew she was picking up a pebble and aiming it towards her mouth.

"Emily, NO!" cried Dawn, dashing to her. She reached Emily just in time to grab the pebble away. "Don't put things in your mouth," she said firmly. Then, for good measure, she added another, "NO!" She certainly didn't want Emily to choke on something.

Goodness, thought Dawn. Aren't two-year-olds supposed to be over that business of putting things in their mouths? Yes, they are, she told herself, realizing something: Emily was not like the other two-year-olds she knew. She thought of Marnie Barrett and Gabbie Perkins, kids us club members sit for. Both Marnie and Gabbie, especially Gabbie, are talkers. (Gabbie's a bit older than Marnie.) Gabbie is toilet-trained and Marnie is working on it. Both girls can put simple puzzles together. When they colour, their drawings are becoming identifiable. And Gabbie has memorized and can sing long songs with her older sister.

Emily, on the other hand, was nowhere near toilet-trained. Her favourite toys were baby toys like stacking rings. When she got hold of crayons, she just scribbled. And her vocabulary consisted of a handful of words and a lot of sounds (such as "buh" or "da") that she used to mean a variety of things.

Yet Emily was smiley and giggly and cheerful. She was affectionate, too, and tried hard to please her new family.

These were the thoughts going through Dawn's mind when Kristy arrived with the Papadakis kids.

"Linny!" shouted David Michael. "Timmy's here! Hey, Kristy, can you coach us? Pretend we're having a Krushers practice, okay?"

"It's okay with me," replied Kristy, "if Dawn doesn't mind watching Hannie, Sari, and Emily. Is that okay with you, Dawn? I'll take the boys and you take the girls?"

"Fine with me," replied Dawn.

So they split the kids up.

Dawn faced Hannie, Sari, and Emily. She didn't know the Papadakis kids very well. "What do you want to do?" she asked Hannie.

"Mmm." Hannie looked thoughtful. "Let's play Ring Around the Roses. I've just started teaching Sari that game."

"Okay," said Dawn. She had recently learned that the actual title and words to the song were "Ring a ring o'roses", but she knew that no little kid ever said that, so she didn't bother to correct Hannie.

"Come here, you two," said Hannie to Emily and Sari, already organizing the game. "Hold my hands. Dawn will hold your other hands . . . Your name is Dawn, right?" she added uncertainly.

"Right," replied Dawn, smiling.

They formed a circle—Dawn, Emily, Hannie, and Sari.

Hannie began the song, singing it as she'd heard it. "Ring around the roses. A pocket full of posies. Ashes! Ashes! We all fall . . . DOWN!"

Hannie and Dawn sat down dramatically in the grass, pulling Emily and Sari with them. Sari giggled. Emily looked startled at first, but then laughed.

"Again!" cried Sari, getting to her feet. "Again, Hannie!" She pulled at her sister's hand.

Dawn and the girls began the game again. The second time, Emily laughed readily as Dawn tugged her to the ground.

The third time, Sari chimed in with, "We all fall . . . DOWN!" And then fell, rolled onto her back, closed her eyes for a moment, and burst into giggles.

The game continued for several more rounds. Each time, Sari picked up more of the song, and then made a big drama out of falling. Emily, however, never said a word. And she rarely remembered to "fall". Dawn usually had to pull her to the ground. Emily seemed to like the game though. She smiled as she walked in the circle, and she giggled as she watched Sari's falls.

When Sari and Emily lost interest in the

game, they let Hannie give them piggyback rides around the garden. Kristy stopped her coaching, and she and Dawn sat in the grass, keeping an eye on the kids and talking.

"I watched you all playing the game," said Kristy to Dawn. "I saw Emily."

"Yeah?" said Dawn, not sure what Kristy was leading up to.

"Emily didn't catch on very fast, did she?"

"Not really," said Dawn carefully, "but I think she had fun."

Kristy just nodded. After a moment she said, "You know what's happened now?"

"What?" asked Dawn.

"Mum and Watson tried to get Emily into a pre-school group. Just for a couple of hours two mornings a week. But she was rejected."

"What?" cried Dawn.

"The school wouldn't take her. They said she's not ready. She's too far behind the other kids. She has to be toilet-trained, and she has to catch up in other areas as well. I mean, you just saw her and Sari. They're about the same age. Look how fast Sari learned the new game. Emily didn't learn it."

"You sound really worried," commented Dawn.

"I suppose I am," said Kristy. "But I seem to be the only one. Everybody else— Mum, Watson, Nannie, Doctor Dellenkamp,

58

even the teachers at the school—think Emily will catch up on her own, and she's just got off to a rotten start. I wish I could spend more time with Emily, but I'm busy with the Papadakises at the moment."

"Well, don't worry so much," said Dawn. "Trust me, it doesn't do any good. Worrying doesn't solve problems."

Dawn's right, I thought later. Only taking action will solve problems. And that was what I planned to do myself.

7th CHAPTER

Deciding to take action about finding my real parents—my birth parents—was easy. Deciding what kind of action to take was not. By the time we held our next club meeting, I still had no idea what to do—but something Kristy had said forced me to decide to figure out a way to start my search immediately.

The meeting was half over. We were talking, eating popcorn, taking job calls, and—in between everything else—listening to Kristy telling us about Emily.

"We all love Emily to bits," said Kristy. "Even Andrew and Karen do, and they resented her at first. The thing is, she's so *different* to the rest of us. And I don't mean in the way she looks. I just can't help comparing her to everyone else in my family. She's slow. She's more like a baby than a two-year-old. When David Michael was two, he became fascinated with cars and learned to identify dozens of them. And Watson says that when Karen was two she was making up stories, and when Andrew was two he learnt how to answer the telephone. But Emily? Well, every now and then she'll pick up on something that really surprises us. But not often."

I couldn't help it. I began to compare myself to Emily Michelle. She didn't look like anyone in her family, and neither did I. She didn't seem to be as clever as anyone in her family and neither was I. When Janine was in the eighth grade, she took advanced science and maths. She won the first prize in the state science fair. Me? I barely scrape by in ordinary classes, I can't spell to save my life, and I can't fathom entering even a *class* science fair.

And Emily was adopted.

So was I. I was sure of that. So—how should I begin my search?

That night, I finished my homework quickly (probably sloppily, too), so that I could think about how to find my real parents. Emily, I knew, had been adopted through an agency called Love Bundles.

I looked up Love Bundles in the phone book. It was listed! It was a local business. I decided to call Love Bundles the next day.

I have never been so nervous about

61

making a phone call. It was Thursday afternoon. I was free until dinnertime. I didn't even have a sitting job. I was alone at home.

With a shaking hand, I picked up the receiver of my phone. I glanced at the number in the telephone book beside me. I had to dial it four times because my fingers were sweaty and kept slipping.

"Love Bundles," said a pleasant-sounding voice, when I'd finally dialled correctly.

"Um . . . um . . . hello." I almost hung up. Then I gathered my courage and said, "I—I'm adopted and I'm looking for my birth parents. I was adopted about thirteen years ago—"

"Excuse me," interrupted the woman. "I'm terribly sorry, but Love Bundles has only been operating for five years. We're a relatively new business. And we place Vietnamese children only," she added.

"Oh," was all I could think of to say. Then I remembered to thank her, and hung up.

There was no way Mum and Dad could have adopted me through Love Bundles. I put away the white pages and took out Stoneybrook's slim yellow pages. No other adoption agencies were listed. So I went downstairs to the study and found the Stamford yellow pages. Under Adoption Services were listed a whole load of places, some of them not even in Stamford. Well, I couldn't start phoning agencies all over Connecticut. At least not at first. That would be a last resort. Besides, what if I'd been adopted privately (through a lawyer), and not through an agency?

Then a thought struck me. My birth certificate! Wouldn't it say where I'd been born? Of course it would! I had to see my birth certificate. Now, where did Mum and Dad keep it? Oh, yes. Our birth certificates are in the safety deposit box at our bank.

Frantically, I looked at my watch. Usually our bank closes at three. But not on Thursdays. On Thursdays it stays open until seven. Goody! I scribbled a note to my family in case someone came home before I did, dashed into the garage, climbed on my ten-speed bike, and cycled into town. When I reached our bank, I chained my bike to a lamppost outside, and pushed my way through the revolving door.

Now. Where to go? Where were the safety deposit boxes? I had to ask the man at the information desk. He directed me down a short flight of stairs where I found a woman behind a sliding glass door. She buzzed me into her office.

"Hi," I said. "My name is Claudia Kishi. My father is Mr John Kishi. I need to get into our safety deposit box."

"Okay," said the woman. "Just give me the key—and some identification so I can check whether you're authorized to open the box."

All I heard was, "Just give me the key."

Key? What key?

"What key?" I asked.

"The key to the box," replied the woman.

"I thought you had it," I told her.

"I've got one. You—or your father—have another. I need both keys to get into the box," she explained, sounding impatient.

I felt incredibly stupid. For a moment, I didn't know what to do. Then I smacked my hand to my forehead and said dramatically, "Silly me! I can't believe I forgot to bring the key. It's at home. Sorry to have bothered you."

I left the bank. My face was burning.

But I wasn't giving up now. I had another idea. Even though I don't go to a paediatrician any more—I go to a doctor who specializes in "adolescent care"—who would know more about my birth and my history than my former paediatrician, Dr Dellenkamp?

Her office isn't far from the bank, so I hopped on my bike and cycled to Dr Dellenkamp's. On the way, I began to worry. What if the next time my father wanted to get into our safety deposit box (with the key, of course), the lady at the bank told him that I had been there? What would my father think? What excuse could I give him if he asked what I'd been doing?

Then it occurred to me that I couldn't just waltz into Dr Dellenkamp's office and ask her if I was adopted. She wasn't my doctor any more, but she had been until recently, and she might tell my parents or something.

I needed a story and I needed one fast.

I thought and thought. I couldn't come up with anything. Well, actually, I thought of several stories, but no *good* ones. I thought of telling Dr Dellenkamp that Janine had come down with a rare blood disease, and that only the blood from a close relative (her sister) could save her life. But of course if I said that, the doctor would phone my parents immediately to see how Janine was doing.

I thought of telling Dr Dellenkamp that I'd been given a school project—to write my autobiography—and I wanted to start with my birth certificate, and also maybe see my medical records. I knew that story sounded slightly fishy, though, and anyway, Dr Dellenkamp probably couldn't release information like that to a kid.

I sighed. Maybe I could just be very subtle. I could stop in, chat with the receptionist for a while, say I missed my old doctor, and ask to speak to her. Then, when I was with the doctor, I'd casually say something like, "So Doctor D., tell me about when I was born. Was my father a wreck? Did Janine get to come to the hospital to see her new sister?"

That *might* work. Just in case, I decided I would have a backup plan. Maybe the school project wasn't too far fetched after all. At least I could ask to see my birth certificate.

Okay. I was ready.

I parked my bicycle in front of Dr Dellenkamp's office and chained it to a bike rack. My heart began to pound as I turned the knob on the glass door that read PAEDIATRIC OFFICES.

I stepped inside and walked to the reception desk. The woman on duty recognized me straight away and I recognized her. Her name is Miss Wilson.

"Hello, Claudia!" she said, sounding a bit surprised. "What brings you here? We haven't seen you for over a year."

Things were off to a good start.

"Hi!" I replied. "I just dropped by for a visit. I kind of miss this place. Oh, and also I need some information for a school project. I need to talk to Doctor Dellenkamp."

"I'm sorry, Claudia, but she's with a patient now," Miss Wilson told me. "Can I help you with anything?"

"Gosh, I don't know," I replied. "I wanted to ask her a couple of questions about when I was born—and maybe see my medical records or something. It's for a school project," I added in a rush.

Miss Wilson looked at me oddly. She paused. Then she frowned. Finally she said,

"Claudia, Doctor Dellenkamp wasn't your paediatrician when you were born. I thought you knew that. You didn't start seeing her until you were about two and your sister was about five."

I frowned back. Talk about fishy stories. How come I didn't remember that? How come no one had told me before?

"Who was my first paediatrician?" I asked, narrowing my eyes.

"Goodness, I'm not sure," said Miss Wilson. "I'd have to ask the doctor if I could check your old records."

"Oh, no. That's okay," I said quickly. "Never mind." That would be going a bit too far for a simple school report. It might cause Dr Dellenkamp to call my parents. I changed tactics and smiled brightly. "Oh, well," I said. "I tried. Maybe I can interview my parents for the—the report. My teacher likes interviews. Thanks, Miss Wilson. 'Bye!"

I left hurriedly, hoping Miss Wilson wouldn't even remember to tell the doctor that I'd been there.

I pedalled home, thinking over what had happened that afternoon. And the more I thought, the more I became convinced of something. Miss Wilson had lied to me. She was covering up . . . a secret.

8th CHAPTER

The next Monday afternoon I was back at Kristy's home, watching Emily and David Michael while Kristy babysat for the Papadakis kids. This time *I* had travelled home on the school bus with her.

It had been a while since I'd had that . . . opportunity. How did Kristy do it twice every weekday? I wondered. It was awful. The sixth-grade boys tormented the sixth-grade girls, and everyone seemed to have the remains of their packed lunch with them. Only they didn't eat it, they threw it around.

"I'm used to it, I suppose," said Kristy, as a pickled onion sailed over our heads. She watched it land in the aisle, and then went on to a different subject, as if the flying onion didn't exist.

I was glad to get off the bus.

Kristy headed for the Papadakises', and I

headed for her house. My sitting job started pretty much the way Dawn's had the week before. Nannie left, Emily whimpered, David Michael arrived, and Emily stopped crying.

But this time, David Michael didn't invite a friend over. In fact, Timmy Hsu called and invited David Michael to *his* house, so I was left alone with Emily.

"Well," I said, looking into her deep dark eyes. "What shall we do today, Miss Emily?"

"Boe!" exclaimed Emily, pointing across the kitchen at absolutely nothing. She grinned at me.

What *were* Emily and I going to do all afternoon?

Emily wandered into the study and I followed her. She found a box of crayons and a pad of paper, plopped onto the floor, and began scribbling. I remembered what Kristy had told us sitters at the BSC meeting: that the pre-school teachers had said Emily wasn't ready to go to school yet. She was still too far behind the other children.

"Hey, Emily," I said suddenly. "Show me the *red* crayon." I was wondering exactly how much Emily did know—and if maybe I could teach her a few things.

Emily just looked at me.

I tried something easier. I knew Emily could follow simple instructions. "Give me a crayon, please," I said.

Very carefully, almost delicately, Emily pulled a blue crayon from the box and handed it to me.

"Good *girl*!" I exclaimed, making a really big deal out of it. "Good girl! Thank you!"

Emily beamed. She loved the attention. She gave me another crayon.

"Oh, *thank* you!" I said. Then I added, "Now this time, give me the *red* crayon."

Emily frowned slightly. Then she smiled again—and handed me the purple crayon, followed by the yellow one.

Okay, so Emily didn't know her colours yet. She certainly couldn't say their names and she couldn't even identify them. I would have to try something simpler. I let Emily go back to her scribbling while I found a pair of scissors and some coloured paper. I cut out two big blue squares, two big red squares, and two big yellow squares.

When I had finished, and the scissors had been put away, I said, "Hey, Emily, let's play a game!" I laid three squares, one of each colour, on the floor in front of Emily. She immediately abandoned her crayons. Then I handed Emily the second red square. "Look," I said. "Here's a *red* square. Can you find the other red one?" I showed her the three on the floor. Then, since I knew that Emily had no idea what we were doing, I pointed to the red square. As soon as Emily picked it up, I praised her as if she'd just achieved world peace or something. I even tickled her, which made her giggle and kick her feet. Then I settled her down, spread out the three squares again, and this time gave her the second yellow one.

"That's *yellow*," I told her emphatically. "Where's the other yellow square?"

Emily handed me the red one again, since she'd received such praise for that before.

Hmm. This was going to be harder than I'd thought.

I tried something new. I mixed up the three squares, arranged them in a different order, and gave Emily the second red square again.

"Emily, that's *red*," I said. "Where's the other red square?"

Emily looked uncertainly at the squares in front of her. The red square had been in the middle before. Her hand went towards the middle square again, which was now the blue one.

"Give me red, Emily," I said, before she could make a mistake. "Give me the one that's the same."

I realized something. I wasn't teaching Emily colours. I was teaching her how to *match*. Was this what being a teacher was all about? Guiding someone towards something, step by step? It wasn't easy. I began to have a little more respect for the teachers at SMS, especially *my* teachers, who probably had to work harder with me than they did with most other kids.

Emily was looking at all the squares in front of her.

I decided to give her some help. Gently, I pulled her hand forward. I placed her red square next to the yellow one, then next to the blue one, and finally next to the red one.

"There it is!" I cried, as we matched the two red squares. "*There's* the one that's the same." I held the squares up for Emily. "They're both red! They're the *same!*"

I could practically see a light go on in Emily's head. Her eyes widened. "Buh!" she said.

I mixed up the three squares again. Before I could even ask Emily to find the red one, she held it up triumphantly.

Whoa! I think I felt as proud as Emily did. I rewarded her with a hug and a cracker. Then I tried changing tactics. I took away her red square and asked her to match the yellow one. After just two false tries, Emily understood what we were doing. She matched the blue one like a pro, and soon the game was too easy for her. I had to make it more difficult.

I added other colours.

Then I changed to shapes (all red, so that the game wouldn't be *too* confusing). Emily could match! Wait until Mrs Brewer came home!

I checked the time. We still had another twenty minutes together, and Emily hadn't lost interest in what we were doing. I decided to go back to teaching her colours, so I put away the shapes and spread the red, yellow, and blue squares in front of her again. This time I didn't hand her a square to match with, though. I just said, "Emily, show me *red*." And then I gave her a hint. I pointed to the red one for her. When Emily picked it up—hugs!

We were still playing the colour game when Mrs Brewer came home from work. Emily had been so intent on her colours that she didn't even see her mother at first. When she finally glanced up and realized that Mrs Brewer was standing in the doorway to the study, she leaped to her feet and gave her mother a tight squeeze around the legs.

"Hi, Mrs Brewer," I said, standing up. "Emily and I were playing some matching and colour games this afternoon." I was about to add, "Do you want to see what Emily can do?" when Emily pulled her mother into the room and began showing off.

Mrs Brewer was impressed. Then she said the last thing I would have expected. "Claudia, how would you like to work with Emily for a while? Maybe twice a week—at your house? I think that going to a new environment and working with someone she doesn't live with would be good for Emily. It would be like going to school."

Me! A tutor? I couldn't believe it! I'm

usually the tutee. But of course I said "Yes", without even hesitating. Then Mrs Brewer and I worked out the arrangements.

When Dad picked me up on his way home from work, I was ecstatic!

9th CHAPTER

Monday evening

I just love sitting for the Perkins girls! They are such great kids. I never know what to expect when I go to their house -- except that something fun or funny or nice will happen. And tonight's sitting job was no different from any other. Before Mr and Mrs. Perkins went out, they gave Myriah and Gabbie permission to "cook with real ingredients," which the girls had asked to do. I wasn't sure about a cooking project, but the end result was a surprise -- a nice one.

The bigger surprise came later, and it involved Chewy. What a wild dog he is. But he's lovable, too. You lot, here's a hint, though : NEVER LET CHEWY NEAR CHOCOLATE-CHIP COOKIES....

Stacey had an even bigger surprise than Chewy that evening (so did I), but she was wise enough not to mention it in the BSC notebook. Everyone would have read about it, and I didn't want that. The big surprise had to do with my adoption.

Anyway, Stacey arrived at the Perkinses' at six-thirty, just as they were finishing an early dinner. Mr Perkins was on his way to see a client (he's a lawyer), and Mrs Perkins was going to choir practice. She has a beautiful voice and sings with a group that has performed all over Connecticut, and also in New York City and Washington, D.C.

"Mummy," said Myriah, as her parents were getting ready to leave, "can Gabbie and I cook with real ingredients tonight?"

Myriah is five and a half, and very bright. Gabbie is two and a half, and also very bright. The girls are famous in the neighbourhood for memorizing and singing long songs. Myriah even goes to dancing lessons. She and Gabbie have a baby sister, Laura, who's just a few months old.

"Cook with real ingredients?" repeated Mrs Perkins uncertainly.

"Puh-*lease*?" said Myriah and Gabbie at the same time.

"I suppose so," replied their mother. "As long as you clear up afterwards and are in bed by eight-thirty. Is that a deal?"

"Deal!" cried Myriah and Gabbie.

Mr and Mrs Perkins gave Stacey some instructions about Laura, and then Stacey said, "Excuse me, but what *is* 'cooking with real ingredients'?"

"Oh," said Mrs Perkins. "The girls can use anything they find in the kitchen—milk, flour, chocolate chips, eggs, whatever —and concoct something. Just do me two favours."

"Okay," said Stacey.

"Make a list of any ingredients they use up so I can replace them, and keep an eye on what they put in their creation. Don't let them eat it if it looks too awful."

"Okay," replied Stacey dubiously. She was uncertain about this project. What if the girls wanted to use a dozen eggs? What if they mixed up something disgusting—like milk and vinegar—and insisted on tasting it? But the Perkinses didn't seem worried, so Stacey decided not to worry, either.

Mr and Mrs Perkins left then, and Stacey settled herself in a kitchen chair with Laura in her arms.

"What do you think your sisters are going to make?" Stacey said to the baby. She held her tight, thinking. There's nothing like the feel of a baby in your arms. She leaned over to smell Laura's baby-smell: milk and powder and soap.

"We're going to make chocolate-chip cookies," announced Myriah.

"No," said Gabbie. "Let's make a green mess."

"A green mess?" said Stacey.

"Yes," replied Gabbie firmly. "You need lots of food colouring for that."

"But you can't *eat* a green mess," spoke up Myriah. "Wouldn't you rather make cookies? Then we can eat them. I want to bake chocolate-chip cookies."

"Don't you need a recipe?" asked Stacey.

"Nope," replied Myriah.

Oh, well, thought Stace. They're just playing.

Gabbie finally agreed to make chocolate-chip cookies, as long as they were green. So Myriah expertly got out flour, vanilla, butter, sugar, an egg, baking soda, chocolate chips, and green food colouring. For someone who was just playing, she certainly seemed to know what she was doing.

Then the girls began to mix the ingredients. Myriah gave instructions and Gabbie followed them, while Stacey held Laura and looked on, making sure that nothing that didn't belong in cookies was added to the dough.

Myriah seemed quite confident in her work, and she didn't even use measuring cups or spoons. She just added things at random, tasted the dough occasionally, and then would say, "I think we need more flour, Gabbie," or, "Just a little more sugar."

As they worked, they talked. "Know what, Gabbers?" said Myriah. "My friends Dana and Fiona are going to day camp this summer."

"What's 'day camp'?" asked Gabbie.

Myriah tried to explain.

Gabbie looked thoughtful. Finally she said, "Be careful of roses. They have horns on them. They'll prick you."

"Thorns, not horns," Myriah corrected her sister. "And what do roses have to do with day camp?"

Gabbie shrugged.

"Here," said Myriah. "It's time to stir in the food colouring and the chocolate chips. Then our dough will be ready." Myriah handed a small bottle and the bag of chips to Gabbie, who gleefully dripped in some green colouring, and then poured a mountain of chocolate chips into the mixing bowl.

Stacey looked round the kitchen, which was pretty messy, and then down at Laura, who had fallen asleep.

"I'd better put your sister to bed," said Stacey to Myriah and Gabbie. "Can you clear up while I do that?"

"Of course," said the girls, and Myriah added, "Then can we bake the cookies?"

Bake them? Green cookies? Stacey hadn't counted on that. She thought the girls were just messing around. "I don't know—" she began.

"Please?" said Gabbie.

"Please?" said Myriah. "It only takes ten minutes to bake chocolate-chip cookies."

"Let me think about it while I put Laura to bed," replied Stacey. "You start clearing up, okay? But don't touch the oven."

So Stacey carried the sleeping Laura upstairs. The Perkinses had moved into Kristy's old house, and Laura's room was the one that had been David Michael's. Stacey laid Laura (who was already in her sleepsuit) in the cot on her tummy, turned out the light, and tiptoed downstairs.

The girls were still clearing up the kitchen. Stacey helped them. When everything had been put away, Stacey inspected the dough. She couldn't taste it because of her diabetes, but it looked surprisingly good, even if it was green. So she and the girls dropped it in spoonfuls onto baking trays and baked it in the oven—for ten minutes, as Myriah had suggested.

When the timer went off, Stacey opened the oven door. The cookies were green, of course, but otherwise looked terrific. "You two are great bakers!" exclaimed Stacey. "I can't believe you didn't follow a recipe."

"Can we each have one before we go to bed?" asked Gabbie.

"Of course. Just let them cool down first. While we're waiting, let's go upstairs and you can put your pyjamas on."

Myriah, Gabbie, and Stacey had been

upstairs for about five minutes when they heard it . . . *CRASH!*

"Uh-oh," said Myriah. "I bet that was Chewy."

"Chewy? I thought he was outside," said Stacey. (Chewy, short for Chewbacca, is the Perkinses' black Labrador retriever. He's the friendliest dog in the world. He's also the most mischievous.)

"He *was* outside," said Myriah, "but we had to let him in while you were putting Laura to bed."

"He was crying at the door," added Gabbie. "He sounded so sad."

Stacey and the girls rushed downstairs. Stacey's heart was in her mouth. What on earth were they going to find? What had Chewy broken?

They ran through the living room. It looked fine.

They ran through the dining room. It looked fine.

Then they reached the kitchen.

One tray of chocolate-chip cookies had been knocked to the floor. The tray lay upside down under the table, and cookies were scattered everywhere. Chewy was standing on his hind legs, about to go after the second tray.

"Chewy! No!" cried Stacey.

Chewy looked around as if to say, "Oh, hi everybody. I was just about to, um, . . . well,

I wasn't going to *eat* these cookies, if that's what you think."

"Don't let him get to the cookies!" said Myriah frantically. "Chocolate is bad for him."

Stacey grabbed Chewy by the collar and led him out to the garage. "Sorry," she told him as she left him there, "but this is for your own good." She returned to the kitchen, helped the girls clear up and throw away the batch of cookies that had landed on the floor, and then let them each eat one from the other batch.

"Yummy!" exclaimed Myriah.

"Green!" said Gabbie.

Stacey read *Green Eggs and Ham* to the girls (Gabbie's request), and put them to bed. Then she went downstairs. In the playroom, she looked through the girls' bookshelf. The Perkinses have a friend who's an editor at a company that publishes children's books, and the friend sends them books all the time: everything from cloth books for Laura, to books that are too long even for Myriah.

Stacey browsed through some of the longer books and came across one with an interesting title: *Find a Stranger, Say Goodbye*. It was by an author named Lois Lowry—and it was the story of an adopted girl, Natalie Armstrong, and her search for her real mother!

Stacey couldn't believe it. She flicked through the book. Then she phoned me.

"Claud!" she exclaimed. "You'll never guess what I've found. I'm sitting for the Perkinses and they have this book. . . ."

Stacey told me what she'd read, and I nearly fainted. I just *had* to get a copy of the book for myself.

10th CHAPTER

When Stacey phoned, I wrote down the title and the author of the book she'd found. I even made her spell out the author's name so I was sure I had the correct information. I make a lot of mistakes, but I didn't want to make any with the book.

"*Find a Stranger, Say Goodbye*," Stacey repeated.

"Find a stranger," I said slowly as I wrote it down, "say goodbye. I wonder what that means. It sounds sort of sad, doesn't it?"

"Yeah," agreed Stacey.

"And the author is?"

"Lois Lowry."

"Just a sec. Lois?"

"Right. L-O-I-S. And her last name is L-O-W-R-Y."

"Okay. Thanks, Stace. This is going to be important. I just know it is."

The next day I arrived at school early so I

could get to our library before registration began. The librarian was surprised to see me, and no wonder. Needless to say, I don't spend a lot of time in the library.

I was desperately hoping to find the book there—and not just because I wanted to get my hands on it fast. You see, I was hoping *not* to have to look for it at the public library. There was too good a chance of running into my mother there. Or of one of her librarian friends saying to her, "You know, Claudia was in today and she took out *Find a Stranger, Say Goodbye*." No, I couldn't let that happen.

Luckily, it didn't. Our school library carries two copies of the book, so I took one out. I spent Tuesday and Wednesday reading it secretly—during study hall, during a boring social studies lesson (I hid the book inside our text), after school, and even in bed with a torch when I was supposed to be asleep.

This wasn't easy. I am not a fast reader (unless I'm reading a Nancy Drew mystery), but I'd made my way through the entire book by 11:30 on Wednesday night. As I read the last word, I said, "Whew!" and closed the book. Done. I needed to do a lot of thinking—but not until the next day. I was too tired just then. I fell asleep immediately.

But on Thursday, I woke up thinking,

thinking, thinking. The story had given me lots of ideas. It had made me feel quite sad, though, too. You see, in this book, Natalie Armstrong's adoptive family is very open with her. And when she says she wants to find her real mother, her parents give her all the information they have about her adoption, which had been privately arranged— and then let her search. They even hire a car for her to use. (Obviously, she was older than I am.)

Why couldn't my parents be so open with me? Why couldn't they be like Natalie's family? Or like the Brewers? I bet my parents wouldn't admit I was adopted even if I found my real mother, brought her home, and introduced her to everyone.

Oh, well. At least I had some ideas for continuing my search. Unfortunately, I had to wait until Friday to take the next step. That was because the next step involved going to the public library (this time I couldn't avoid it), and I had to wait until my mother would be busy so she wouldn't see me. Every Friday afternoon, Mum conducts a staff meeting in the conference room on the second floor of the library. I needed to use one of the microfiche machines on the first floor. So I timed my library trip to coincide with the staff meeting.

The meetings always begin at three-thirty. At 3:35, I was parking my bike outside the library. At 3:36, I was walking up the stone steps and through the double front doors. The first thing I did was check to see who was at the main desk. Good. It was just a student volunteer. I hoped I'd find another student volunteer helping out with the mircrofiche machines. The students don't come in often enough to know that I'm Mrs Kishi's daughter.

I wound my way past the information desk, and around the periodical section to where I wanted to be. And a student was on duty! Great luck. I'd never even seen him before. Maybe this was a sign that I'd discover something important.

It was. I did discover something important—but completely unexpected.

"Excuse me," I said to the student.

He looked up from a book he was reading and peered at me through thick glasses.

"Yes?" he said. "May I help you?"

"I hope so," I replied. "I need to see some old birth announcements in the *Stoneybrook News*. And—and I need you to show me how to use a microfiche machine. I mean, if it isn't too much trouble."

"No trouble at all. That's what I'm here for. Which issues of the paper do you want to look at?"

I decided to look at the announcements for the week in which I'd been born as well as the next two weeks—just in case it had taken a while for the announcement to appear.

The boy set me up at a machine and showed me how to scan the material in the newspaper. Then he left me on my own.

I quickly found the birth announcements for the week in which I'd been born. There were quite a few names I knew. They were kids I go to school with. My name wasn't there.

I looked through the next two weeks' announcements. No Claudia Kishi. Or Claudia anything. Puzzled, I returned to the boy at the desk. I asked to see the *next* month, and then, on a hunch, asked to see the month *before* I'd been born. Was it possible that my birthday wasn't really my birthday? That I'd been born a few weeks earlier, but because of some muddle with the adoption papers I'd been listed as being born on another date?

At that point, anything seemed possible. So I looked over two more months of announcements.

No Claudia.

I sighed. This meant that one of several things was true. I'd been adopted through an agency. I'd been privately adopted—but not born in Stoneybrook. Or I'd been adopted and born in Stoneybrook, but my real mother had given me another name. Then Mum and Dad had legally changed it to Claudia. Either way . . . *I was adopted*. All birth announcements automatically go to the local paper. And no Claudia Kishi was listed.

I let the news sink in.

Then I took a deep breath and went back to the list of babies who'd been born the week in which I thought I'd been born. I would have to track those babies down. It was a good starting place, anyway. I couldn't go looking for every baby born that entire year.

Ten babies had been born that week—six boys and four girls. I eliminated the boys straight away. That left the girls. One of them was named Francie Ledbetter. I eliminated her, too. She goes to SMS with me. I was down to three girls. Was I one of them? Had my parents adopted Kara Ferguison or Daphne Selsam or Resa Ho? None of those babies had a Japanese last name (and I couldn't ignore the fact that I *am* Asian), but I decided that didn't matter much. Not every Japanese person has a Japanese last name. Or maybe my real mother was Japanese and my real father was American, and I had my mother's features and my father's last name. Who knew?

I took a pencil and paper out of my bag. Very carefully, I copied down the names of the three baby girls and their parents:

Kara Ferguison, born to Mr and Mrs Jim Ferguison of Rosedale Road.

Daphne Selsam, born to Mr and Mrs Terrance Selsam of High Street.

Resa Ho, born to Mr and Mrs George Ho, visiting from Cuchara, Wyoming.

That third baby, Resa Ho, intrigued me. First of all, Ho is an interesting last name. Isn't there a Hawaiian singer named Don Ho? Could I be Hawaiian or Polynesian, not Japanese? Maybe. Second, the paper said Resa's parents were "visiting from Wyoming". Were they really just visiting? Or had they come to Stoneybrook to have the baby because they already knew they couldn't keep her, and my parents had arranged to adopt her? I didn't know if private adoptions worked that way, but it seemed possible. And were the Hos really from Wyoming? Or were they from Hawaii or California or a place where there are a lot of Asians or Polynesians? Not that there aren't Asians in Wyoming, but the Hos might have been protecting their identity. In fact, maybe their last name wasn't Ho at all. Maybe it was Hoshikawa or Hoshino, or even Yamaguchi or something.

Now I was getting somewhere.

I was also getting scared.

So I phoned Stacey as soon as I returned from the library.

"Stace?" I said. "Would you like to stay after the meeting tonight? You could have dinner with us, and then we could talk. *Really talk*. We haven't done that for a while."

"Claud," Stace replied, "what's up? I know something's up."

"Just talk to me tonight. That's all."

And so, because Stacey is my best friend, she agreed to without asking again about what was going on. She knew she'd find out when I was ready to tell her.

11th
CHAPTER

Stacey stayed for dinner. No one in my family thought that was unusual. Nor that Stacey came up to my room for a gossip afterwards. We do both of those things pretty often.

At first we just talked about school and boys and things. For nearly half an hour we talked about this one boy, Trevor Sandbourne, whom I used to like a lot. And all the time, I could almost *see* Stacey wondering what I really wanted to talk about, because she knew it wasn't Trevor.

So at last I drew in a deep breath and said, "Well, I read *Find a Stranger, Say Goodbye*. From cover to cover."

"You did?" asked Stacey, being careful not to push.

I nodded. "And after I'd read it, I had some more ideas for my search. You know how, in the book, Natalie Armstrong is privately adopted? I mean, through a lawyer, not through an agency like Emily Michelle was?"

"Yeah," replied Stacey.

"Well, maybe I was privately adopted, too. I might even have been born right here in Stoneybrook to a couple—to a really young couple—who knew they weren't ready to bring up a child. So they planned, before I was born, to have me adopted by a family who wanted a baby. Maybe Mum and Dad found out they couldn't have any more children after they'd had Janine or something."

"Like my parents," said Stacey.

"Right," I agreed. "So d'you know what I did today?"

"What?" Stacey leaned forward eagerly.

"I went to the public library and looked up old birth announcements."

I told Stacey everything that had happened and what I'd learned.

"It sounds a bit far-fetched," Stacey said, when I'd finished my story. She was frowning slightly. "I mean, what if you *were* adopted through an agency? Or what if you were adopted privately, but not here in Stoneybrook? You could have been born anywhere."

"I know," I answered. "But it proves one thing. I *was* adopted. If I'd been born to Mum and Dad, the announcement would have been in the paper. That's just the way it goes. All births are listed. *And mine wasn't.*"

"True," said Stace slowly.

"And there's a *chance* I was born in Stoneybrook. It certainly would have been easy to adopt me that way. Then my parents wouldn't have had to travel here with a newborn baby."

"That's true, too," said Stacey.

"So you know what?" I went on. "I think I'm going to look up those three couples. That would be a starting point, anyway. I just don't know how to do it."

"The parents' addresses were in the paper, weren't they?"

"Yeah," I replied. "But that was thirteen years ago."

"So? Your family has lived in this house for more than thirteen years. And the Pikes have lived in theirs for a long time, too. And until recently, Kristy and Mary Anne lived in the houses they'd been born in."

"Right. . . ."

"So get out the Stoneybrook phone directory," said Stacey excitedly.

"I'm nervous!" I cried, but I found the book anyway. I was as excited as Stacey was.

I closed the door, and Stacey and I huddled together on the bed.

I looked up the Ferguisons first. Mr and Mrs James Ferguison of Rosedale Road were listed—right there on the page in front of us.

"I don't believe it!" I cried. I jotted down their phone number.

Next I looked up the Selsams. They were not listed.

"Oh," I said dispiritedly.

"Don't give up yet," said Stacey brightly. "You've still got their address. Maybe they're just ex-directory."

"Oh, right!" I said, feeling hopeful again.

Then, although it seemed completely unnecessary, I looked up the Hos. Of course, they weren't listed.

"Well, you've got two leads," said Stacey. "You can phone the Ferguisons, and you can go to the Selsams'. You can cycle to their house. It isn't too far away."

"True." I reached for the phone. Then I looked at my clock. "Drat!" I said. "It's after ten. I'd better wait till tomorrow to call the Ferguisons."

"And I'd better go home!" exclaimed Stacey, jumping up.

"My mum will drive you," I told her. "Come on."

So I saw Stacey to the door, and then I went back to my room.

Tomorrow I would contact the Ferguisons and the Selsams. I was so nervous I knew I would hardly be able to sleep that night.

I was right. I barely slept a wink on Friday night. When I woke up on Saturday, my eyes felt as if they were made of sandpaper

—all scratchy. But I was ready for action, and I was wound up as tightly as a spring.

I couldn't believe my luck. By ten-thirty that morning, Dad had gone into town to run errands, and both Mum and Janine had left for the library—Mum to work on a fund-raising project, Janine to research something scientific and complicated.

As soon as they had left, I made a dash for the phone in my room. I wouldn't even have to close my door or keep my voice down. Once again, luck was on my side.

Still, the phone call wasn't going to be easy to make. I had a story all dreamed up—I'd thought of a good one while I'd been lying awake the night before—but I had butterflies in my stomach like you wouldn't believe. This was worse than stage fright. My whole past was at stake here.

But putting off the call wouldn't make it any easier, so I picked up the phone and dialled the number. A man answered.

"Hello, Ferguison residence," he said. I assumed it was Mr Ferguison.

"Um, hello," I said. "My name is Claudia. I live here in Stoneybrook. And, um, I'm really sorry to bother you, but at school, we're supposed to be doing a research project—on names. I was given the name Ferguison because of its unusual spelling. I decided to do something with a family tree." (I knew this sounded vague, but I was hoping the man would humour me in order to get off the phone quickly.)

"Yes?" said Mr Ferguison.

"Well, I was wondering if you have any kids. I mean, so I can include them in the tree. I just need to know their names and their birth dates. Do you have kids?"

"Yes, I do," replied Mr Ferguison. "Kara, Marcie, and Joseph." He told me when they'd been born. Kara had been born in the week I'd been born.

I pretended that this was a great coincidence. "Hey!" I exclaimed. "What do you know? I'm thirteen, just like Kara. I wonder why I don't know her. We must be in the same grade." (I wanted to be *sure* of Kara Ferguison's existence.)

"Do you go to Stoneybrook Day School?" asked Kara's father.

"Oh, no," I replied. "I go to the middle school. I suppose that explains things. Well, thanks for your help. I really appreciate it. I need to get a good mark for this project.

Mr Ferguison laughed. Then we said goodbye and hung up.

One down, two to go. It was time to head for the Selsams'. Again, thanks to my sleepless night, I had a story all ready as to why I was appearing on their doorstep.

When I reached their house, I realized I wasn't quite so nervous as when I'd called Love Bundles or the Ferguisons'. Maybe I was getting used to being an undercover detective.

I rang the doorbell boldly.

A woman answered it. She was young and pretty. A little boy peered timidly around her.

I pretended to look confused. "Mrs Selsam?" I said.

"No," replied the woman, looking confused herself.

"Oh," I said. "I didn't think so. I'm sorry to bother you. You see, I used to live in Stoneybrook, but my family moved away. Now we're back for a visit. I'm looking for my best friend from kindergarten. We haven't been in touch. Her name is Daphne Selsam. I know she used to live in this house."

The woman smiled. "The Selsams were the previous owners," she said. "They live in Lawrenceville now. That's not too far away. Maybe someone could drive you over there. In fact, I think I've even got the Selsams' phone number. Can you hold on a minute?"

Of course I could!

The woman left, returned with a slip of paper, and handed it to me.

"Thanks!" I cried.

I cycled home and called the Selsams without a single butterfly. This time I told the woman who answered the phone the same story I'd told Mr Ferguison—about a school project.

And I found out that there was indeed a Daphne Selsam who was thirteen.

That left just one baby unaccounted for: the baby born to the Hos from Cuchara, Wyoming—if that was their real name, and if they really were from Wyoming.

But how would I track *them* down? I had run out of ideas. My mind had been working overtime. Still, I planned to look for them. I thought I might wait a while, though. The real search was getting a bit intense.

I was glad when Stacey phoned. "How's it going?" she asked.

"I've been playing detective all morning," I told her. "Can I come round? I'll fill you in."

"I wouldn't miss it for the world," Stacey replied. "But do you mind a lazy afternoon? I'm feeling a bit tired today. So Mum said I have to stay on bed."

"*On* bed?" I repeated.

"Yeah. That means I'm allowed to be dressed, and I can get up when I really need to, but mostly I'm supposed to rest."

"Well, I'll come and entertain you," I said. "I'll tell you what happened, and I'll bring over some art supplies. We can make jewellery. That won't be too taxing."

"Great!"

I cycled to Stacey's and spent the afternoon with her. It was nice to have a break from my search.

12th
CHAPTER

monday

This afternoon, sibling rivalry reared its ugly head. (Isn't that a great phrase? "Reared its ugly head"? I read that somewhere.) Anyway, the siblings are David Michael and Emily. The rivalry part is that my brother is jealous of his sister because of all the attention she's been getting lately. It is true that Emily's been getting a lot of attention, but she needs it. She's having some trouble, and all the things we're doing -- sending her to work with Claudia, seeing doctors, etc. -- are necessary. But David Michael just knows that we don't have as much time for him as we used to. So when I sat for him this afternoon, I tried to be very positive and upbeat with him. It helped, too. Boy, did it help!

"Kristy, where's Nannie taking Emily *now*?"

That was the first thing David Michael asked Kristy when she began her sitting job with him. It was a Monday, several weeks after I'd started working with Emily Michelle, and Kristy was in charge of David Michael. Her mum and Watson were at work, of course, her older brothers had after-school activities, and Nannie had just driven off with Emily.

"She's taking Emily back to the pre-school group," Kristy replied.

"Why?" David Michael demanded. "And why's she doing it *now*? School's over. It's after three-thirty." (David Michael is very proud of the fact that not only can he tell the time, but he has his own watch.)

"Nannie's taking her back to be re-evaluated," said Kristy.

"Huh?"

"The teachers agreed to test Emily again. Mum and Watson think she's made a lot of progress since Claudia began tutoring her. If she has, the teachers might let her start going to school."

"Oh." David Michael kicked at his book bag, which he'd dropped in the front hall when he'd come home that day.

Kristy noticed that, but all she said was, "Come on. We've got a Krushers' practice today, and we're going to have to walk to the playing field. Home, too. Charlie can't drive us."

"Okay," mumbled David Michael.

Kristy and her brother changed into their Krushers T-shirts. Then Kristy got her equipment together, remembered to put on her collie baseball cap, and she and David Michael set off.

The walk to the playing field is quite a long one, and David Michael was silent for at least half the journey. When Kristy couldn't stand it any longer, she said, "Okay, out with it."

"Out with what?" asked David Michael, his eyes to the ground.

"Out with whatever's bothering you. Come on. Tell me what's wrong."

At first David Michael didn't speak. Then he blurted out, "I hate Emily!"

"You hate her?" Kristy repeated mildly.

"Well, I suppose I don't hate her. But—but she gets so much attention!"

"Hmm," said Kristy. "You know, sometimes I feel jealous of Emily, too." (That was a very clever thing for Kristy to say. She didn't just *accuse* her brother of being jealous; she simply appeared to assume he was jealous and that she took it for granted, and then she admitted to being jealous herself. She didn't make David Michael feel defensive or guilty about anything.)

"You *do*?" said David Michael, awed.

"Oh yes," said Kristy. "She takes up time with Claudia, who's *my* friend, and Mum and Watson talk about her nonstop."

"Yeah." David Michael sounded angry.

"So you know what I do?"

"What?"

"I tell myself two things. One—that Emily really *is* having problems and she *does* need help, and that Mum and Watson would pay a lot of attention to *me* if *I* ever needed help. And two—that there are a lot of things I can do that Emily can't. Just think," Kristy went on. "If you were Emily, you couldn't play softball. You couldn't read. You couldn't watch your favourite TV programmes because you wouldn't be able to understand them. You couldn't go to birthday parties—"

"I wouldn't have friends," David Michael continued, "and I couldn't ride my bike or go skateboarding."

"That's right. You know what? I love Emily. I really do. But I think you're terrific, too. You're nice to your friends. You're funny. You like animals. And you're a good big brother to Karen and Andrew and even Emily."

"Am I a good ballplayer?" asked David Michael.

Kristy couldn't lie. "You're getting an awful lot better," she replied, and that seemed to satisfy her brother.

The thing about the Krushers is that they really aren't very good ballplayers. That was why Kristy started the team in the first place. She knew there were a lot of kids in

Stoneybrook—boys *and* girls—who were either too embarrassed to join Little League, or too young. So she started her team for those kids. And what she ended up with was a bunch of players who can barely play—but who have more enthusiasm for the game than you'll find anywhere. They try hard, they're very supportive of each other, and they hardly ever get discouraged. In fact, they're so hardworking that they've come close to beating Bart's Bashers a few times. The Bashers are another team that, like Kristy's, aren't in Little League. The difference between the Bashers and the Krushers, though, is that the Bashers are older than most of the Krushers—and they're good. One interesting point—Kristy and Bart Taylor go out together sometimes, even though they coach opposing teams. They're not boyfriend and girlfriend (yet), but I have high hopes for this.

Anyway, by the time Kristy and her brother reached the playing field that day, David Michael was feeling pretty cocky from all the compliments Kristy had paid him. And it showed later during the practice.

"Okay, team!" Kristy shouted, clapping her hands together.

The ragtag Krushers gathered around their coach. There were Myriah and Gabbie Perkins (Gabbie, you'll remember, is only *two and a half*); Jamie Newton, who ducks every time a ball comes towards him; Max Delaney and Hannie and Linny Papadakis, who can barely hit the ball; Jackie Rodowsky (the walking disaster); Matt Braddock, who's deaf; and a bunch of other little kids, including Timmy Hsu, who had just joined the team. Guess who else was there—The Krushers' cheerleaders! They are Vanessa Pike, Charlotte Johanssen, and Haley Braddock.

The practice began. Kristy separated the Krushers into two teams and chose David Michael to pitch for his side. Then she gave the Krushers a pep talk: "Now get out there and play your hardest! We've got a big game against the Bashers coming up!"

First up to bat was Hannie Papadakis. David Michael pitched unusually well that day. Hannie struck out.

Myriah stepped up to the plate, swung at David Michael's first pitch, hit the ball, and made it to second base.

Everybody cheered for her, even the kids on the other side. That's just the way the Krushers are.

Then it was Claire Pike's turn to hit. Kristy exchanged a glance with the cheerleaders. Immediately they launched into, "Krush those Bashers! Krush those Bashers!" to encourage Claire.

But Claire struck out. And as everyone had feared, she threw a tantrum. "Nofe-air!

Nofe-air! Nofe-air!" she shrieked, growing red in the face.

Vanessa is used to her sister's tantrums. She took her aside, calmed her down, and returned her to the batting queue. Claire didn't have another chance to hit in that inning, though, because Jackie Rodowsky was up next and he struck out, too.

"Okay, change sides!" yelled Kristy. (She thinks this is nicer than yelling, "Three strikes, you're out!" Or, "Three outs!")

The batters took their places in the ball field, and Kristy lined up the other players in their batting order.

The new pitcher was a boy named Jake Kuhn. David Michael was the first up to bat. He swung at Jake's pitch, and . . . *CRACK!* He hit a home run!

"Way to go, David Michael!" Kristy shouted.

And the rest of the kids screamed and jumped up and down.

When practice was over, David Michael's side had won. His teammates (well, all the Krushers) gathered around him, slapping him on the back and telling him how well he'd played.

"Maybe I'm ready for Little League now," said Kristy's brother.

"Oh, no! You can't leave us!" said Timmy Hsu.

"Yeah, the Krushers *need* you," added Max Delaney.

David Michael couldn't help grinning. "I'll stay for another season," he said as the kids started to leave for home.

Kristy and her brother had just got ready to leave, too, when someone tapped Kristy on the shoulder.

She turned round.

She found herself facing Bart Taylor—and she nearly had a heart attack.

"Bart!" she exclaimed, heart thumping.

"I thought I'd find you here," said Bart.

"Are you spying on the Krushers?" teased Kristy.

"Of course not. I just wanted to walk you home." Bart slipped his arm through Kristy's.

David Michael looked on. Kristy could tell he felt left out again, so she linked her other arm through David Michael's. "I'm pretty lucky," she said. "I've got *two* handsome boys to walk me home." (And she had two handsome boys to help her to carry the equipment.)

David Michael beamed.

When Kristy and her escorts reached the Brewer mansion, Kristy was all ready to invite Bart to come in for a while—but just then Nannie's car pulled into the drive.

"Bart," said Kristy quickly, "I have to go. I'll explain later. Thanks for coming to practice. I'm really glad you did."

Bart is pretty easy-going, so he left. No questions asked.

Kristy made a beeline for Nannie. "What did the teachers say? What did the teachers say?" she asked as Nannie unbuckled Emily from her car seat.

"Oh, darling," said Nannie. "We won't know for a while. The teachers need several days to go over the test results."

"Oh." Kristy was disappointed. But hopeful. She said to me later, "Claud, I've got faith in you. I'm sure you've helped Emily. You can do almost anything."

Boy, did I hope she was right.

13th
CHAPTER

The day after Kristy's Krushers' practice, Charlie brought Emily over to my house for a tutoring session. Honestly, Charlie ought to go into the chauffeuring business. He could probably make a fortune.

"Hiya, Miss Emily," I said as I opened the door and Charlie put Emily down on our front steps.

"Hi, Ko-ee," replied Emily. She smiled. Emily was beginning to greet people and to call them by name, and she pronounced the names as well as she could.

"Thanks, Claud," said Charlie. "I'll be back for Emily in about an hour, okay?"

"Perfect," I replied. "See you."

"'Bye, Emily," said Charlie as he started going down the steps.

"'Bye, Shar-ee." Not a whimper from Emily. She'd been to my house plenty of times by then and knew that Charlie (or someone) would come back for her. Her fears were starting to disappear.

"Okay, Emily," I said, ushering her inside. "Let's go up to my room."

We always worked in my room. I had decided to follow a routine with Emily, just as if she were at school and always went to the same classroom.

So we trudged up the stairs to the second floor. (Emily is not a very fast stair-climber.) We passed Janine's room.

"Hi, Nee-nee!" called Emily cheerfully.

Who could resist that? Not even Janine.

"Emily!" my sister exclaimed, and handed her a balloon, which she'd obviously been saving for Emily's next visit.

"What do you say?" I whispered to Emily.

"Fank-oo," she answered promptly.

Then, never missing a teaching opportunity, I said, "Emily, what colour is your balloon?"

"Bwow up!" replied Emily.

"Yes, but what *colour* is it?"

"Red. Bwow up!"

Since she was right, I blew it up immediately. Then we continued down the hall and into my room, where I settled Emily on the floor. I put the balloon on my desk. "You can have it when Charlie comes back," I told Emily. (If I let her play with it, she'd never be able to concentrate.)

For the next hour, Emily worked hard.

By now, she was an old pro at matching, could name quite a few colours, and could identify shapes. She couldn't say the words for the shapes, though. Most of them were just too hard. Once, I asked her to say "triangle" and she looked at me as if I was mad.

Today's lesson, I had decided, would be on counting. From watching *Sesame Street*, Emily already knew how to count to ten, but the words didn't mean anything to her. She'd just reel off (very fast), "One-two-fee-foe-five-sick-seben-eight-nine-ten." Now I needed to show her what those words meant.

I placed three blue triangles on the floor in front of Emily.

"Bwoo!" she said.

"That's great, Em," I told her. "They are *blue*, and they are all the same—they're *triangles*—but *how many* are there?"

Before Emily had a chance to get frustrated, I took her finger and pointed to each one, saying clearly, "One . . . two . . . *three*!"

"Foe-five-sick-seben-eight-nine-ten!" continued Emily triumphantly.

"No, let's start again."

So we did. I added another triangle and we counted to four. That afternoon we counted circles, squares, Emily's fingers and toes, my shoes, some pencils, and finally—just as Charlie was arriving—we counted one piece of chocolate, which I gave to Emily as a reward for her hard work. She was definitely not a counter yet, but she was on her way.

When Emily had left, I quietly closed the door to my room. I could hear the clickety-clack of Janine's computer and knew she was hard at work, and probably a million miles away (mentally), but I wasn't taking any chances. I had decided to call Wyoming, and I didn't want Janine to overhear.

It had taken me a long, *long* time to find the nerve to make the Wyoming call (or calls), and now I was ready. If I didn't call, I'd never find out about Resa Ho, and I'd really regret that one day. I was pretty sure of it.

I got out the phone book. I looked up the area code for Wyoming, hoping desperately that there would be only one. There was. It was 307. I didn't pause. I plunged ahead and dialled (307)555–1212.

"What city, please?" asked the operator.

"Cuchara," I replied.

"Okay, go ahead."

Go ahead? Oh. She meant what number did I want.

"I need the phone number for the Hos."

"The Hos?"

"Yes, Ho. H-O."

"There are three Hos in Cuchara, ma'am," said the operator patiently. "Do you know the party's address or first name?"

The *party*?

"Um, is there a George Ho?" I asked.

"I'm sorry, I have no such listing."

"Oh. Well, could you give me the numbers for the three Hos that you do have?"

The operator then gave me the numbers for a Mary Ho, for Sydney and Sheila Ho, and for Barry and Patty Ho.

"Thank you," I said, and hung up.

I just kept forging ahead. I dialled Mary Ho first. The phone rang twelve times. No answer. She wasn't at home.

Next I tried Sydney and Sheila Ho. A woman answered on the first ring! And then—I swear, I don't know *where* this idea came from—I found myself saying, "Congratulations! Your daughter Resa has been chosen as the winner in the—"

"Excuse me," said the woman, "but I don't have a daughter named Resa. My daughter is Pamela."

"Is she thirteen?" I asked briskly.

"Yes."

"Hmm." I pretended to be puzzled. "Do you know of a thirteen-year-old girl in Cuchara whose name is Resa?"

"No." The woman sounded irritated.

"That's a shame," I said. "I mean, about your daughter. She would have been the winner of a twenty-one-inch colour television and a video recorder."

Then I hung up. I called Barry and Patty Ho and tried the same trick. But the boy who answered the phone said he was

113

fourteen and had two younger brothers.

I tried Mary Ho again. Still no answer.

Then I dialled Stacey. "Guess what?" I said. "I've found my real mother."

"You're kidding!" Stacey sounded astonished.

I explained what had happened when I'd called Wyoming. I said that by the process of elimination, Mary Ho must be my mother.

After a long pause, Stacey said, "Claudia, believe me when I say this. I really think you may be adopted. But I do *not* think that Mary Ho is necessarily your real mother. In the first place, you didn't talk to her. For all you know, she's only twenty-one years old. In the second place, what makes you so sure you were born in Stoneybrook?"

"I don't know," I said. "It just seems logical. Once I heard a news story about a woman who gave birth to a baby she couldn't keep, so the doctor who delivered the baby adopted him. *That* baby would have been born in the same town where his birth mother had lived. Anyway, think about it. I'm like *no one* else in my family. I even look different. I think maybe I'm only half-Asian. I think—" I began to cry.

"Claud, slow down. You're jumping to all sorts of conclusions. Look, everyone is different, and not everyone fits into his or her family. I'm the only McGill with diabetes. And think how different Jessi

114

and Becca Ramsey are. And look at Nicky Pike, for heaven's sake. Talk about not fitting into your family. His brothers tease him and he doesn't like to play with his sisters."

I sniffed. "I suppose you're right," I said.

"The thing is," Stacey went on, "you're not going to feel better until you know the truth. You don't even know for *sure* that you're adopted."

"But how am I going to find out? I don't know how to search any more."

"Ask your parents," said Stacey flatly.

"They'll never tell me the truth."

"Why are you so convinced of that? They told you the truth when Mimi was ill. They've told you the truth about plenty of things. *Ask them*. You have to confront them."

I let out a shaky breath. "Okay," I said. "I'll talk to them after dinner."

14th CHAPTER

Think it was tough waiting until after dinner?

Well, you're right.

But it had to be done. Mum and Dad came home from work and they were starving, so my family ate dinner together straight away. And I wasn't going to bring up the subject of my adoption in front of Janine. I needed to have a private talk with my parents. My *adoptive* parents, that is.

Dinner was almost painful. Those butterflies were back, and I could hardly eat. I couldn't concentrate, either. I kept saying, "What? What?" Mum asked me twice if I was feeling okay. She even leaned over and felt my forehead. When Janine dropped her fork, I jumped a mile. I nearly fell out of my chair. At that point, I saw Mum and Dad exchange a glance, which of course was about me.

All during dinner I'd wondered how to ask my parents for a private conference, but in the end, I didn't have to ask. They asked me. First they said, "Janine, will you clear up the kitchen tonight, please?"

"But it's Claudia's turn," Janine replied.

"You're swapping for tonight," said Dad in his no-nonsense voice. "Claudia will clear up tomorrow."

"*Okay*," replied my sister, pouting.

Then Mum said, "Let's go into the study, Claudia. Your father and I want to talk to you."

They *did*? Were they going to say they knew what I'd been up to—my search and everything—and they'd decided to tell me the truth?

No.

We settled ourselves in the study, Mum and Dad on the couch with me between them. A Claudia sandwich with parent bread.

"Claudia," said my father, "something is obviously very wrong. Your mother and I couldn't help noticing your behaviour at dinner. We hope you'll talk to us and let us try to help you."

I nodded. A big lump in my throat kept me from speaking.

"Are you having trouble at school?" asked Mum gently. She brushed a strand of hair from my face.

I shook my head.

"It isn't report time," said Dad, trying to make a joke.

I couldn't even smile.

"Did you have a row with Stacey?" asked Mum.

Again I shook my head. And then (I couldn't help it) I began to cry.

My parents were truly alarmed.

"Claudia?" said Dad.

"You *lied* to me!" I finally said in a tight whisper.

I didn't see it, but I knew that Mum and Dad were frowning at each other over the top of my head.

"We lied to you?" repeated Dad.

"Yeah," I said with a little gasp. "All these years. All the times when you said, 'When Claudia was born . . .' or, 'When Claudia was a baby . . .' or, 'When Claudia came home from the hospital . . .' And not one of those times—*not one*—did you say I came home from the hospital as an adopted baby."

"An adopted baby!" exclaimed my mother.

"Yes. I know all about it. I found the clues. Everything makes sense. There are hardly any baby pictures of me and there are tons of Janine. *Tons*," I added for emphasis.

"But—" said Dad.

"And I'm so different from you two and Janine. You're all clever and you're sort of—what's the word?—conventional. And

118

I do badly at school and I'm a wild dresser and maybe a little bit boy-mad. And I don't even look like the rest of you."

"But—" said Mum.

"Also," I rushed on, "I found the locked cash box. In there," I said, pointing to the desk. "I wasn't snooping. Honestly. I was looking for more baby pictures when I couldn't find enough in the photo albums. I know my adoption papers are in that box."

"But—" said Dad.

"And last of all, the final proof," I continued, "is that there's no birth announcement for me in the *Stoneybrook News*. I went to the library and I used the microfiche machine to check. So I know I wasn't born here. Or if I was, my real mother gave me a different name. So now I want you to please tell me the truth. Come on. I can take it."

My parents looked shocked. That's the only way to describe their faces. I bet they didn't think I was bright enough to figure things out.

"Come on," I dared them again.

"Claudia, dear," said Mum. "You are *not* adopted."

She said it so simply that I believed her straight away.

"I'm not?"

"No," she and Dad replied at the same time.

"You mean I'm your real child?"

"Of *course*." Dad took my hand.

"But what about the pictures?" I asked.

Mum looked embarrassed. "I'm sorry, honey, but we have no explanation for that except that you are our second child. It's just a sad fact that there are usually more pictures of a first baby than of a second one. Parents are awed by their first baby. They can't believe what they've created. So they can't stop taking pictures. But when the second child—or the third or fourth or fifth—comes along, they're more used to things. And they don't have as much time for picture-taking because the new baby isn't their only child. They're a lot busier."

I relaxed a little.

"As for being different," said Dad, "believe me, everybody is different. And think how boring a family would be if all the people in it were alike."

"Think of Peaches and me," added Mum. "Who would ever guess we're sisters? You know, *you* and Peaches are very similar."

"And Janine may look like me," said Dad. "I know that's what you've been thinking. It's hard not to notice that, but you're a pretty good cross between your mother and me. And believe it or not, you look very much the way Mimi did when she was young."

"I do?" I almost began to cry again.

"Yes," said Mum, looking tearful herself. "I'll show you some old pictures of Mimi later."

120

I relaxed even more.

"Now," said Dad, "would you like to know why your birth wasn't announced in the *Stoneybrook News*?"

"Yes," I answered. "Very much."

"Because it was announced in the *Stoneybrook Gazette*. So was Janine's birth."

"The *Stoneybrook Gazette*? What's that?"

"A local paper that went out of business about nine years ago."

"If you went back to the library and looked at the *Gazette* on the microfiche machine, you'd find your announcement," said Mum. "But you won't have to bother with that, since I have a copy of the entire paper in the desk in my bedroom."

"Oh, wow!" I said. I actually laughed. Mum and Dad smiled.

"Feel better?" asked my father.

"I'll feel completely normal as soon as you show me what's in that box in the bottom drawer of the desk."

Dad didn't hesitate. He stood up, strode to the desk, removed the box, took his keys out of his pocket, and unlocked the box. He held it open in front of me.

It was full of money.

"Oh, my lord!" I cried. "What that for?"

"Emergencies," Mum told me. "There are five hundred dollars in that box. And *nothing else*. We'd appreciate it if you wouldn't tell anyone that, though. We wouldn't want to be robbed. The money is there in case we ever need fast cash in the middle of the night."

I slumped onto the couch. "I don't believe it," I said softly. "I feel so stupid. *You* must think I'm stupid."

"Of course we don't," said Dad. "We think you're bright and sensitive and creative. And different."

I smiled.

"And we like you just the way you are," added Mum. "We also know that thirteen is a difficult age. I suppose you have an even tougher time than most kids, though—trying to keep up with a sister like Janine."

"That's for sure."

"Well, we want you to know," said Dad, "that in the future, we'll try to pay more attention to your feelings."

"And I want *you* to know," I said, "that I'm really, really sorry I accused you of lying to me."

Mum and Dad smiled. Then we hugged.

And then, of course, I had to go to my room to phone Stacey.

Later, Mum found the pictures of Mimi. We compared pictures of Mimi at twelve with pictures of me at twelve.

We could have been twins.

That night, I slept with one of the pictures of Mimi under my pillow.

15th
CHAPTER

It was Friday, three days after I'd found out that I wasn't adopted after all. I was waiting for my friends to arrive for the day's BSC meeting. While I waited, I stared at the wall over my desk. Something new was hanging there. I'm always painting pictures or creating things to hang in my room, and I change them regularly.

The new thing, though, wasn't one of my creations. Well, not really. What I had done was take one of the pictures of twelve-year-old Mimi, and one of my seventh-grade school pictures, mounted them, and framed them side by side in a single frame. I knew I would never take that down. It was something that would hang in my room until I went away to college (if I could get into any college), and then it would go with me so I could hang it over the desk in my college room.

I was so intent on gazing at the photos that I didn't hear Stacey come into my room.

"Oh, wow!" she said softly, looking at the pictures. "That's you and Mimi, isn't it?"

"Yes," I replied, trying not to let Stacey know that she'd just taken about ten years off my life by sneaking up on me.

"Well, I don't think there's any question that you're Mimi's granddaughter, do you?"

"Nope. And if Mimi were alive, she probably would have found these pictures for me the very night I discovered the locked box, and then my search wouldn't have happened at all."

"Probably," agreed Stacey. "I suppose we just have to learn to get along without some of the people we love, though." (I knew she was thinking of her father and the divorce.)

"Gosh, this is a cheery conversation," I said.

Stacey laughed. Then she flopped onto my bed. "I'm exhausted," she said. "All I did this afternoon was sit for Laura Perkins, and she slept most of the time. You'd think I'd just run a marathon. Dawn's going to have to take the desk chair today, because I claim a place on the bed."

I looked critically at Stacey. She was *always* tired these days. She was too thin, and half the time she didn't feel well.

"Stacey—" I began, about to give her a lecture, but just then Kristy burst in.

"Hi, you two!" she cried. She settled into the director's chair, put on her visor, and stuck a pencil over one ear.

During the next five minutes, Jessi arrived, then Mal, and finally Mary Anne and Dawn. All the BSC members were present.

Kristy called us to order. "Any club business?" she asked.

"I move that we have a snack," I said.

"I second the motion," added Mallory.

Kristy tried to frown, but couldn't. "Okay," she said. "Claud, pass around whatever you've got hidden in here, and then I have some news. Some *club* news," she said pointedly.

I pulled a bag of mini-chocolate bars from under the quilt at the end of my bed, and a bag of crisps from behind my pillows. While my friends helped themselves, Kristy said, "Okay, here's all sorts of news. First, Mr Papadakis—I mean, Hannie and Linny and Sari's grandfather—is leaving the nursing home tomorrow. He's over the pneumonia, and his hip is healing just fine."

"That's great!" said Dawn and Mary Anne.

"Yeah!" agreed the rest of us.

"I know," said Kristy. "I have to admit I'm going to miss that regular job, though. The Papadakis kids are so nice. I really like them. You should have seen what they made their grandfather to welcome him back to his house."

"What?" asked Jessi.

"A welcome-home card that's taller than Linny."

"You're kidding!" cried Stacey.

Kristy shook her head. "Nope. They worked hard on it, too. Even Sari. Mrs Papadakis had given them lots of materials —paper doilies, cotton wool, glitter, stars, you name it. Linny drew big letters that spell out 'WELCOME HOME, POPPY', Hannie coloured them in, and Sari glued things anywhere she felt like it. The card is actually quite funny-looking. There are glue drippings *every*where, things falling off the edges, and every time the kids pick the card up, glitter showers off it. But they're really proud of their work."

"That's really sweet," I said.

"Yup. Anyway, one good thing about the end of the job with the Papadakises is that now I'll have more time to spend with Emily. Which brings me to my next piece of news," said Kristy. "The teachers gave Mum and Watson the results of their re-evaluation of Emily."

I glanced around my bedroom. Every single one of us had leaned forward. On the floor, Jessi in her jeans and ballet leotard, and Mal in a new sweater dress, were leaning forward. On the bed, Stacey in her

New York sweat shirt, Mary Anne in one of Dawn's baggy T-shirts, and me in a Day-Glo-striped top and skintight leggings, were leaning forward. And on the desk chair, Dawn, wearing an outfit of Mary Anne's, had cocked her head towards Kristy. (She couldn't lean forward or the chair would have fallen over.)

"The news," said Kristy, "is good."

The six of us let out sighs of relief and relaxed a little.

"The teachers say that Emily has made a *lot* of progress," Kristy began. "First of all, she's not so afraid of everything. She trusts people more. She knows that when she's left somewhere, or even just left alone in her room, someone will come back for her. She's still not crazy about thunderstorms or the dark, and she still cries out in the night sometimes, but she's better about both things."

"What about school?" I asked, sounding like a nervous parent.

"The teachers are positive that Emily will be able to start preschool in the autumn," Kristy answered. "That's fine with us. She'll be three then, which is the age Andrew and Karen started preschool. Also—"

Ring, ring!

"I'll get it," said Dawn. She picked up the phone. "Hello, Babysitters Club. Dawn Schafer speaking." (A pause.) "Oh, sure. I'll get straight back to you. 'Bye."

Dawn hung up, and we arranged for a sitter for the Delaneys, who live in Kristy's neighbourhood. We had to call on our associate members, though, since all seven of us were busy that afternoon. Luckily, Shannon Kilbourne could take the job.

The phone rang a couple more times then, and we got busy with our calendar and schedules. Kristy was beaming. She loves busy meetings.

The meeting finally settled down, though, and Kristy finished telling us about Emily. "One thing we'll have to do this summer is get her toilet-trained," she said. "But I think Emily will manage that. The best part, though, is that the teachers can't believe the progress Emily has made in terms of skills. You know, learning her colours and stuff. And *that*," she went on, "is due to you, Claud."

I grinned. I felt so proud. I, Claudia Kishi, the not-so-great eighth-grade pupil, was a teacher! A good one. I could teach kids things, and teach them so well that real teachers were impressed!

"Remember how worried you were about Emily?" Jessi said to Kristy.

"Yeah." Kristy looked a bit sheepish. "I think I was more worried than I needed to be. Mum and Watson and the doctor and the teachers kept saying Emily would be fine. I was afraid something was really wrong. Thank goodness everyone else was right. They knew what they were doing. Oh, you know what else the teachers said?" Kristy was looking at me.

"What?" I asked.

"That you should keep working with Emily. Mum wants to talk to you about that. You don't have to turn her into Super-Baby, but your tutoring sessions are good preparation for real school."

"Wow! They really want *me* to work with her?"

"Yup. I suppose I could do it, or Nannie could. But Mum says it's good for Emily to get close to people outside the family. Besides, you're doing a great job."

"Thanks! I suppose I ought to call your mum. We haven't arranged Emily's next session. Do you think your mother's home from work yet?"

Kristy looked at my clock. "I don't know. It depends. She might be. Try phoning her, okay?"

"Okay." I reached for the phone and dialled the Thomas/Brewer number.

After three rings, I heard a fumbling noise at the other end. There was a pause. Then a voice said cheerfully, "Heyyo!"

Oh, my lord! Emily had answered the phone. "Emily? It's Claudia."

"Hi, Ko-ee."

"Hi!" I put my hand over the receiver. "You lot! You won't believe this. *Emily* answered the phone!"

Kristy looked shocked. Then she grinned. "Let me talk to her."

I handed her the phone. "Hi, Emily! It's me, Kristy." Kristy paused, smiling. Then she looked at the rest of us and announced, "Emily just said, 'Heyyo'."

Well, of course when that happened, everyone else wanted to talk to Emily on the phone. It wasn't until the last of us had finished talking that I said to Kristy, who was holding the receiver, "Do you think your mother's there? Someone must have helped Emily get to the phone, and I still need to talk to your mum to arrange the next tutoring session."

Kristy giggled. "I forgot about that." After asking Emily about five times if she could please talk to Mummy, she finally reached Nannie, who said that Kristy's mum wasn't at home but that she'd phone me that evening.

It was after six by then, so my friends left. I stayed in my bedroom. I sat at my desk and stared up at the photos of Mimi and me. "I can't believe I thought I was adopted," I said to Mimi's picture. "But you have to admit, the clues were there. And Emily Michelle and I *do* have a lot in common. But I am so, so, so glad I'm your real granddaughter. I mean, your family-related-blood kind of granddaughter. And I'm glad Mum and Dad are my real parents. I'm even glad Janine is my natural sister. I really am."

I stood up, turned off my light and walked down the hall to Janine's room. "Let's make dinner together tonight," I said to her. "We'll surprise Mum and Dad. It'll be fun."

Janine looked at me in surprise. Then she said, "Okay." But first she had to save some material on her disks and switch off her computer. When that was done, she smiled at me.

My sister and I went downstairs together.

THE BABYSITTERS CLUB

Need a babysitter? Then call the Babysitters Club. Kristy Thomas and her friends are all experienced sitters. They can tackle any job from rampaging toddlers to a pandemonium of pets. To find out all about them, read on!

MYSTERY THRILLERS

Introducing a new series of hard-hitting action-packed thrillers for young adults.

THE SONG OF THE DEAD by Anthony Masters
For the first time in years "the song of the dead" is heard around Whitstable. Is it really the cries of dead sailors? Or is it something more sinister? Barney Hampton is determined to get to the bottom of the mystery . . .

THE FERRYMAN'S SON by Ian Strachan
Rob is convinced that Drewe and Miles are up to no good. Where do they go on their night cruises? And why does Kimberley go with them? When Kimberley disappears Rob finds himself embroiled in a web of deadly intrigue . . .

TREASURE OF GREY MANOR by Terry Deary
When Jamie Williams and Trish Grey join forces for a school history project, they unearth much more than they bargain for! The diary of the long-dead Marie Grey hints at the existence of hidden treasure. But Jamie and Trish aren't the only ones interested in the treasure – and some people don't mind playing dirty . . .

THE FOGGIEST by Dave Belbin
As Rachel and Matt Gunn move into their new home, a strange fog descends over the country. Then Rachel and Matt's father disappears from his job at the weather station, and they discover the sinister truth behind the fog . . .

BLUE MURDER by Jay Kelso
One foggy night Mack McBride is walking along the pier when he hears a scream and a splash. Convinced that a murder has been committed he decides to investigate and finds himself in more trouble than he ever dreamed of . . .

DEAD MAN'S SECRET by Linda Allen
After Annabel's Uncle Nick is killed in a rock-climbing accident, she becomes caught up in a nerve-wracking chain of events. Helped by her friends Simon and Julie, she discovers Uncle Nick was involved in some very unscrupulous activities . . .

CROSSFIRE by Peter Beere
After running away from Southern Ireland Maggie finds herself roaming the streets of London destitute and alone. To make matters worse, her step-father is an important member of the IRA – if he doesn't find her before his enemies do, she might just find herself caught up in the crossfire . . .

THE THIRD DRAGON by Garry Kilworth
Following the massacre at Tiananmen Square Xu flees to Hong Kong, where he is befriended by John Tenniel, and his two friends Peter and Jenny. They hide him in a hillside cave, but soon find themselves swept up in a hazardous adventure that could have deadly results . . .

VANISHING POINT by Anthony Masters
In a strange dream, Danny sees his father's train vanishing into a tunnel, never to be seen again. When Danny's father really does disappear, Danny and his friend Laura are drawn into a criminal world, far more deadly than they could ever have imagined . . .

POINT HORROR

Introducing a new series of horror fiction for young adults
– read them if you dare!

APRIL FOOLS by Richie Tankersley Cusick
Driving back from a party on April 1st Belinda, Frank and
Hildy are involved in a gruesome accident. Thinking no
one could have survived, they run away from the scene.
But someone must have survived the crash, and they're
going to make Belinda suffer for what happened . . .

TRICK OR TREAT by Richie Tankersley Cusick
From the beginning Martha knew there was something
evil about the house; something cold; something sinister.
Then the practical jokes begin, and she is sure someone is
following her . . .

MY SECRET ADMIRER by Carol Ellis
Jenny's parents go away leaving her alone in their new
house. Then the phonecalls start – Jenny has a secret
admirer who courts her with sweet messages, but she also
has an enemy who chases her on a lonely road. She has no
one to turn to except her secret admirer – but who is he? . . .

THE LIFEGUARD by Richie Tankersley Cusick
Kelsey's summer on Beverley Island should have been
paradise, but it quickly turns into a nightmare. It starts
with a message from a girl who's missing, and there have
been a number of suspicious drownings. At least the
lifeguards will protect her. Poor Kelsey. Someone forgot to
tell her that lifeguards don't always like to save lives . . .

BEACH PARTY by R.L. Stine

Karen plans to party all summer with her friend Ann-Marie. The fun starts when she meets two new guys. But which should she choose: handsome Jerry or dangerous Vince? But the party turns nasty when the threats start. Someone wants Karen to stay away from Jerry at all costs . . .

FUNHOUSE by Diane Hoh

Everyone in Santa Luisa is horrified when the Devil Elbow's roller coaster flies off its rails. And no one believes Tess when she says she saw someone tampering with the track. But someone knows Tess is telling the truth – someone who is playing a deadly game, and Tess is in the way . . .

THE BABY-SITTER by R.L. Stine

From the moment that Jenny accepts the Hagen baby-sitting job, she knows she's made a terrible mistake. The Hagen house fills her with horror, and she finds a creepy "neighbour" prowling in the back yard. Then the crank phonecalls start – but who wants to hurt her? What kind of maniac is willing to scare her . . . to death? . . .

Look out for:
Teacher's Pet by Richie Tankersley Cusick
The Boyfriend by R.L. Stine